THE BLIND WRITER

INTERSECTIONS

Asian and Pacific American
Transcultural Studies

DAVID K. YOO
RUSSELL C. LEONG
Series Editors

The
BLIND WRITER
❧ *Stories and a Novella*

Sameer Pandya

University of Hawai'i Press
Honolulu
*in association with the UCLA Asian American
Studies Center, Los Angeles*

Printed in the United States of America

20 19 18 17 16 15   6 5 4 3 2 1

Library of Congress Cataloging-in-Publication Data

Pandya, Sameer, author.
  [Prose works. Selections]
  The blind writer : stories and a novella / Sameer Pandya.
        pages cm—(Intersections)
  ISBN 978-0-8248-3958-1 (cloth : alk. paper)
  ISBN 978-0-8248-4798-2 (pbk. : alk. paper)
    1. East Indian Americans—California—Fiction. I. Title. II. Series:
Intersections (Honolulu, Hawai'i)
   PS3616.A368A6 2014
   813'.6—dc23

                                                                2014023237

Journal Acknowledgments
"Patrick Ewing's Father" in *Narrative Magazine* (2005)
"Welcome Back, Mahesh" in *Other Voices* (2005)
"M-o-t-h-e-r" in *Epiphany Magazine* (2007)
"Ajay the Lover" in *Ozone Park Journal* (2011)
"A Housewarming" in *Faultline* (2013)

Statement of Fiction
*This is a work of fiction. Names, characters, places, and incidents either are
products of the author's imagination or are used fictitiously. Any resemblance
to actual events or locales or persons, living or dead, is entirely coincidental.*

University of Hawai'i Press books are printed on acid-free
paper and meet the guidelines for permanence and
durability of the Council on Library Resources.

Designed by George Whipple

Printed by Maple Press

In memory of my father

Oh, what can you do with a man like that?
What can you do?

—JOHN CHEEVER,
  "Goodbye, My Brother"

CONTENTS

THE BLIND WRITER

PART ONE

M-o-t-h-e-r

Uma Shastri had worried about loving her boys too much. But then again, she wondered, what in the world was too much?

In high school and college, Uma was good at math and economics only because she studied so hard. But with a field hockey stick or a tennis racquet in her hand, her body slid to all the right places without conscious thought. With her strong thighs, quick feet, and icy insides, she was always the best player on any field. Later, when she was married, she wanted a daughter but learned to be excited about the boys that came out of her belly. Sure, she could have given a girl the real encouragement in sports she never had, but the boys would be an easier sell. As the years passed, neither boy showed any interest in Little League, tennis, or even Ping-Pong. Instead, they loved chess and, with their sharp memory and an ability to visualize and break down words, were highly skilled spellers. Her husband, Arun, thought spelling and chess were the only sports worth encouraging. She said they weren't real sports; he said they showed spelling bees on ESPN. Once she realized that both boys had genuine interest, Uma decided she'd help them become accomplished, well-known spellers, even though they weren't all that interested in the competitions.

It was just past six a.m. on a Saturday morning, and the family was on the road to the state spelling championships, in Sacramento. They'd allotted two hours' driving time and two more just in case. Arun had suggested they drive the night before and stay at a motel, but Uma said no because all the responsibility would fall on her. Arun would pack a few things in a bag five minutes before they were scheduled to leave. She had to pack for her and the two boys and deal with food. Her elder son, Pankaj, was allergic to dairy and wheat. And so they were on the road at six a.m. Both Uma and Arun liked getting to their destination early, though Uma liked it just a little more.

As soon as they got in the minivan, Pankaj went to the seat all the way in the back and fell asleep. Bankim sat in the first passenger seat. Arun drove, and Uma sat next to him.

Arun and Uma didn't think of driving a minivan as surrendering to a staid domestic life in the suburbs. In fact, they'd actively sought out the life. They spent the first two years of their marriage in Baltimore, where Arun was completing his medical residency. They rented an apartment at a safe distance from the tough neighborhood surrounding Johns Hopkins. Arun spent his days and many nights at the hospital, while Uma had to fend for herself. She had an economics degree but had trouble finding work. She ended up working at a fabric store for minimum wage. The first month, a woman in their apartment complex was held up as she was opening the door to the building. This haunted Uma for the rest of their time in Baltimore. When she ventured out, she did not feel comfortable until she was safely back inside their apartment. When they left Baltimore and headed west, they agreed that they wanted nothing more to do with urban living. They wanted a place where the parking was easy and where they didn't have to spend the thirty yards before the front entry readying the key so that they could open and close the door in one swift, defensive movement. A large, comfortable car was one small part of the life they'd envisioned.

"Don't you want to get a little sleep?" Uma asked Bankim. "You didn't fall asleep until late last night."

"I'm fine," he said, staring out at the empty freeway. One reason Bankim was so good at chess and spelling was that he could sit quietly in one place for hours.

"We have plenty of time. Rest your eyes." She felt more nervous than he did. She'd only had a few short stretches of sleep the night before, and now her eyes and head felt heavy. A lack of sleep shortened the leash on her temper. She closed her eyes for a few minutes.

Some of Uma's best childhood memories revolved around early mornings. When she was young, she, her mother, and her two older brothers often took an early morning train from Bombay into Gujarat to spend time with her mother's family. Uma's mother got them up, dressed, and to the train station while she and her siblings were still half asleep. And then they'd be settled in a train compartment. Even before the train started moving, Uma was fast asleep. She'd wake up a few hours later to a sharp, sunny day, with the countryside moving in a blur of greens and blues. Her mother had a plate of fried snacks and a thermos of hot tea ready. Uma wanted to duplicate the magical sensation of going to sleep in one world and waking up in another, but Pankaj usually slept through all their trips and Bankim never went to sleep.

When they were about half an hour away from Sacramento, Uma called back to Pankaj and woke him up.

Both brothers wore long-sleeved button-down shirts that Uma had ironed for them the night before. Pankaj's shirt was already untucked and completely wrinkled. Two years before, when he was thirteen, Pankaj was pictured on the front page of their local newspaper, with his disheveled chambray shirt, standing with his shoulders slouched and his back in a C, holding up his plaque: "LOCAL BOY WINS STATE SPELLING BEE." At the national bee, he lost in the second round. Both brothers knew that Bankim was now expected to win here and then do better at the nationals. They'd be the first set of brothers to win the same state spelling bee. There was a two-year difference between them, but they looked very much alike. They wore wire-rimmed glasses and had bowl cuts, soft hands, bad posture, and slightly protruding bellies. The only difference was that Bankim didn't wrinkle his shirts, and that might have been the main advantage the younger had over the older.

Pankaj climbed out of the back and sat next to Bankim. "Donkey," he whispered.

Bankim started giggling. They were best friends and each other's spelling partners. In between difficult words, they competed over who could come up with the silliest ones.

"Shh," Arun said, looking through the rearview mirror. "Let Bankim concentrate."

"He's concentrating too much," Pankaj said. "He needs to relax."

Arun didn't say anything for a few seconds. "Maybe that's a good idea. We all need to relax a bit." It had been a quiet and tense ride. Uma had tried but couldn't fall asleep.

"Just sit quietly," Uma said. "We're almost there." She didn't like how Arun let the boys do whatever they wanted. He was too easily swayed by them. Pankaj had made a good point, but she didn't like it when he talked back. He wasn't rude, but he simply no longer assumed that his parents were always right. Bankim was impressionable and looked up to his brother.

"Booty," Bankim whispered.

"B-o-o-d-y."

"Stupid. It's b-o-o-t-y."

By 7:30, they reached the high school where the bee was being held. Though the parking lot was nowhere close to full, there were already quite a few cars. Uma felt a bit of panic but assumed that people had simply arrived early. Arun and Pankaj stayed in the car while she and Bankim went to register.

Ten minutes later, Uma was taking long strides across the parking lot, with Bankim several steps behind her trying his best to keep up.

"Arun, it starts at 8:30, not 10." Uma didn't understand how she had gotten it wrong. She never got such things wrong. She was worried that this was a sign of bad things to come. If she couldn't keep up her end of the bargain, how could she expect Bankim to keep up his?

"It's fine," Arun said, looking at his watch. "We still have over half an hour."

Arun's patients and colleagues always commented on how casual and comforting he was in his bedside manner. But this wasn't the time for it. "I asked you to take care of this one thing. I've done everything else. Why can't you help out a little?" She knew she hadn't asked Arun to keep track of the start time. She was just worn out from everything she'd done to insure the smooth movement of the day. The night before, after they'd all gone to bed, she stayed up well past midnight, making fresh samosas for the trip. When she had offered them during the car ride, they'd all dismissively said they weren't hungry.

Pankaj called Bankim into the car, where he was playing his Game Boy.

"We're fine," Arun said. "Let's not do this in front of them now."

Arun walked to the open side of the car and asked with added cheer, "Are you ready?"

"Sure," Bankim said. "I've been ready for a week."

"Let's go in," Arun said.

"The boys haven't eaten yet," Uma said. "And I don't want to be in the auditorium with all the nervous kids and their parents."

She handed Pankaj his own Tupperware, which had three different kinds of wheat-free and dairy-free snacks. She, Arun, and Bankim ate from a larger container of samosas and pakoras. Samosas and tea before the start of a spelling bee: it was their small version of a tailgate party.

"Are those OK?" Uma asked Pankaj. They'd only recently found out about the wheat allergy, and she was still figuring out how to work around it.

"They're fine," Pankaj said.

Bankim ate two samosas quickly and was going for a third.

"Slow down," Uma said. "You don't want to get a stomachache up there."

Pankaj looked into the canvas food bag. "Where's the ginger ale?"

Uma looked into the bag. She'd packed a thermos of tea and a bottle of cold, sweetened milk for Bankim. She forgot Pankaj's safe drink for road trips.

"I'm so sorry," she said. "I was running around, and I forgot this one thing. I'm really sorry."

"What am I supposed to drink?"

Uma didn't like the tone in his voice. "The tea doesn't have that much milk," she said. Even a couple of tablespoons of milk destroyed Pankaj's digestive system for days.

"That's not funny," Pankaj replied, his voice a little shaky.

"We'll get you a drink inside," Arun said.

She looked at Pankaj, still her little boy with allergies, and thought about apologizing but didn't feel like it.

They finished eating and went inside.

In the auditorium, they wished Bankim good luck: Pankaj squeezed his shoulder, Arun shook his hand, Uma played with his hair and then combed it through with her fingers. By 8:20, Bankim was in his seat onstage, in the first of five rows of seats. Only a few others kids were seated. Many parents were still standing with their kids in front of the stage, hugging and kissing them. Uma hoped that Bankim knew that though she wouldn't be so affectionate in public, she'd be there for him long after most of these parents gave up.

She didn't love one son more than the other, but she and Bankim had an unusual connection from very early on. Pankaj, like his father, had an intellect that scared Uma. They both used it to cut people off in conversation. Bankim, on the other hand, had to work a little harder in school. But he was a charmer. Right now, there was a charm in how his glasses always slipped below the bridge of his nose. Though everyone always wanted to play with him, he would withhold his interest for as long as he could and then give himself to one or two people and only for a limited period of time. Mostly, he'd stay attached to Uma's leg. She'd never known love and devotion in the way she felt it from him.

Arun, Uma, and Pankaj found seats toward the back of the auditorium. Uma wanted a place where she didn't have to make small talk with any of the other parents. Once they sat down, she raised her hand and put it down when Bankim noticed. Now that he knew where they were, Bankim would only look for them if he was in trouble.

At 8:30, the main judge came up onstage and explained the rules to the participants and audience. As he was talking, Uma scanned the stage for competition. She recognized several kids from previous bees but felt confident about Bankim's chances. And then they got started. There were a hundred kids competing, and the first couple of rounds were very slow. They got rid of the underprepared and those who were too nervous to perform in front of crowds. One boy broke into tears before he was halfway through *democracy*. Bankim easily got past the first two rounds with *abdomen* and *ostensible*.

By the time Bankim got up for the third round, an hour had passed. Arun read Ludlum; Pankaj had recently gotten into Asimov. Uma, however, had not taken her eyes off the stage. Arun and Pankaj only looked up when Bankim asked for the word *dungarees* to be pronounced for the second time. In the early rounds, Bankim usually spelled the words quickly, thinking he should save his energy for the later rounds. But with *dungarees,* he was taking a long time.

"What's he doing?" Pankaj asked. "He knows this word. It's easy."

"Shh," Uma said.

Bankim stood casually at the mike with his hands in his pockets. For about ten seconds, he just stood there. Uma quickly scanned the audience. Except for a few whispers here and there, they were all intently watching her son.

Even from where they were sitting in the back, Uma could clearly see Bankim's eyes as they bulged out and then receded. It frightened her. His head swooned back a little, and with his hands still in his pockets, he stumbled like a drunk, took a few steps sideways, and at the last possible moment, took his hands out of his pockets and used them to break his fall. All the kids leaned forward to look, and there was a collective gasp from the audience. Just as Arun and Uma got up out of their seats, Bankim used his hands to get up. He pushed his glasses up his nose with his thumb and middle finger, walked to the mike, spelled out d-u-n-g-a-r-e-e-s correctly, and went back to his seat, as if nothing had happened. For the first several seconds after he sat down, no one knew what to do. It took the audience that time to decide that Uma's cute but dorky thirteen-year-old boy had displayed a great bit of courage

9

and strength when, despite the pain and disorientation he must have felt, he got up and took care of the job he'd come to do. He persevered through pain for the sake of a larger purpose. At first the audience clapped quietly. But when they processed what had happened, seemingly all at the same time, they went wild with their cheering. Everyone stood up and clapped and kept clapping. As the family walked down the center aisle toward the stage, Uma whispered under her breath, "That's my boy." They were clapping for him, but they were also clapping for her, for raising a child who got up when others would have stayed down.

When the family reached the stage, the bee officials had already taken Bankim to the back. The main judge went onstage and said the competition was temporarily on hold.

"What's wrong?" his father asked, placing his hand on Bankim's forehead and cheeks.

"Nothing," Bankim said. He was sitting in a chair, his shirt still neatly tucked in. "I just felt a little lightheaded."

"We have a school nurse, and she's on her way," the judge said.

Arun was about to say that he was a doctor, but the judge walked away.

"Do you feel tired?" Arun checked his son's pulse and looked at his eyes.

"A little."

Arun asked Pankaj to give Bankim some of the cranberry juice he'd bought earlier from the vending machine. Bankim took several sips. Uma ran her fingers through his hair. "How do you feel?"

"Fine," he said.

The nurse, an older woman in street clothes, arrived a few minutes later, checked Bankim's vitals, and asked him some questions. Arun spoke to her but didn't say he was a doctor. She said she couldn't see anything outright that was wrong and that he was fine to go on if he liked. "It's up to you."

Arun and Uma walked to a corner away from the kids.

"What do you think?"

"You know what I think," Uma said.

"Even after what's happened? He's sick. He passed out. We've been pushing him too hard. His body is rebelling against the exhaustion and stress."

"I know you think I'm being selfish, but I'm not. Bankim has worked very hard for this. And he'll want to know why we didn't encourage him to keep going."

"Bullshit," Arun said and looked to see if his kids had heard him. If they had, they didn't turn to look at them. "This isn't encouragement. It's being pushy."

"This isn't about me. I've watched him study." Not only had she watched him, she'd created tests for him to take and study guides for him to use. She'd even found a guy who taught Bankim basic Latin roots. "He doesn't want to lose this opportunity. Look at them. They're going on like nothing has happened." The two brothers were standing around and laughing, as if, indeed, nothing had happened.

The boys were a constant source of disagreement between Arun and Uma. Arun believed in a laissez-faire policy of child rearing. His parents had maintained a distance from their children but had offered advice and emotional support when needed. Arun thought he'd turned out pretty well: he loved his parents, and he'd never cheated on either his wife or his taxes.

"Arun, your father never knew whether your birthday was in April or October," Uma had once said.

"So? He remembered everything that was important."

Arun was comfortable with his father's distance; Uma was trying to make up for the distance she had from both her parents.

"And the nurse said he's fine," Uma said. "You said he's fine."

"OK," Arun said. "Let's at least ask him."

They called Bankim over.

"Hey, buddy," Arun said. "How do you feel?"

"Fine."

"Do you want to keep going?"

Bankim looked at his mother and then his father and then back to his mother. "Yeah," he said.

"Are you sure?" Arun asked.

This time, Bankim just nodded his head.

Arun and Uma went to find the judge. "I still think this is a very bad idea," Arun said.

When Bankim returned to his seat onstage, the audience clapped again, though this time not as loudly. Bankim kept his head down and found his seat. He'd never had this much attention centered on him before. He waited as they went through the rest of the third round. When it was his turn in the fourth, he got up, listened for the word, spelled *regiment* immediately, and returned to his seat, without letting a second pass between each task. And then the words kept coming, and Bankim kept spelling them correctly. *Idiopathic, pharmacology, lumpen, fecundity, odoriferous, pettifog.* The group onstage got smaller and smaller. Uma went to the bathroom when there were still twenty-five kids left and Bankim had just completed a round.

She walked into a stall and sat down. Since Pankaj had been born, she'd used the bathroom for a few stolen moments of quiet, which she now desperately needed. She was relieved that Bankim was on track. When she played tennis, she had an uncanny ability to sense when her opponent was feeling nervous. And right at that moment, she'd attack. Bankim was equally good at the mental game. He didn't think about what came before or what would come after. He went from word to word and stayed within the game. But as much as she loved competition, her constitution couldn't quite handle the pressure when her kids were competing.

A couple of women came into the bathroom a minute after her. They washed their hands and fixed their makeup.

"I'll be glad when it's over," one woman said. "Our lives have been crazy."

"I don't know where Sam gets the strength and motivation," the other said. "He's up in the morning before us."

There was a pause for a few seconds.

"I'm glad that little boy is OK," the first woman said, her voice a little softer then before.

"He's precious."

Uma was happy to hear this.

"But I can't believe he's continuing on. If I was that mother, I'd get him to a doctor and give him a full checkup. What if there's still something wrong?"

Uma wanted to say that nothing was wrong, that her husband had checked.

"It's just irresponsible. I'd be mad too if, after all the work we've done, Michael had to drop out. But I'd understand."

Uma had seen them on TV: mothers who pushed their kids too far, mothers who fought other mothers over who had the better, brighter, prettier, more athletic child. She'd been wondering whether she'd gone too far this time. Bankim could take the pushing, though she needed to be careful. But hearing these women articulate her fears made her feel even more self-righteous. Who the hell were they? They knew nothing about her or her life. Spelling separated her from parents pushing their children to be better football players and bouncier cheerleaders. She was helping them to be smarter, more successful kids. Who didn't want that for their children? Once she had gotten over the disappointment with her boys' disinterest in physical sports, she realized that encouraging them at spelling was very important. Despite the promise that America made about equality, her boys would never get their backs scratched in the same way their white counterparts would. The only recourse they had was to be the smartest in the room. It wouldn't make them equal, but at least it would keep them in the game.

And she encouraged the boys in spelling so that she could spend time with them. She'd gone from a father to a husband. In her boys, she saw a chance to give and receive with some purity. Uma didn't have many friends. She'd lost touch with her school and college friends from India and child rearing didn't leave time to make new ones. But it wasn't really an issue of time. She didn't know how to relate to adults. She was graceful and wore her saris well and made small talk when she and Arun had dinner with his colleagues. But she didn't spend time one-on-one with other women. She didn't act childish, and she didn't want to be a child. But given the choice, she'd rather spend time with children. Adults disappointed her. They insisted on conversations about their anxieties and failures. They said one thing when they meant another. She found children to be straightforward: they smiled when they were happy, cried when they weren't.

Uma had intended to wait until the two women left the bathroom to come out. But occupied by her thoughts, she opened the stall door. All three made eye contact through the large mirror in front of them. Uma was unmistakable. At five ten, she was an inch taller than Arun. And they'd all watched her run down the middle aisle when Bankim fell, her single braid whipping up and down like a snake.

Right when she made eye contact with them, Uma felt calm. She wasn't going to say anything. It was not her place or responsibility. They were the ones who'd been talking, and they'd have to be the ones doing the talking now. Uma walked over to a sink, washed her hands, and wiped them. She looked at one woman and then the other and smiled. "Have a nice day," she said and walked out the door. As she stepped away from the bathroom, she wished she could hear what they were saying now. Her moment of restraint felt like a great victory, as if her restraint, when she had every right to tell them to go fuck themselves, washed away their criticism that she was a bad mother and a bad woman. A bad mother would have insisted on a fight in the girls' bathroom while their kids were outside competing and working hard. No, Uma was a good mother for taking the hit on the chin and moving on.

She walked back to her seat a little tingly, as if things were going to turn out all right.

At the end, there were two: Bankim and an unremarkable young girl named Joan from Stockton who'd not struggled with a single word that day. The auditorium was still full. The audience didn't openly root for one kid over another. But Uma felt that despite what they thought of her, surely they were secretly hoping that Bankim would win. Bankim and Joan went back and forth for seven rounds. Uma couldn't sit and watch. Her stomach was rumbling, and she vowed that this would be the last time she was going to come to one of these events. She had a family history of high blood pressure.

Arun came up to the little hidden corner behind the last row of chairs where Uma was standing. When she first saw him coming toward her, she was annoyed. They stood together for about five seconds before Uma said she was going back to their seats.

"It's fine," he said. "Pankaj is there. He'll take care of him if he needs it."

She hesitated and then stayed put.

Arun stood next to her, holding her pinky finger in his hand and repeating, "He'll be fine, baby." This was Arun's term of comfort and love, used very sparingly.

With Arun holding her pinky, they got through the rounds. As it happens often, Joan got a fairly easy word—*solvent*—wrong. She spelled it with an *a*. According to the rules, Bankim had to spell *solvent* and the next word on the list to win. He began to work it out in his mind. Uma remembered going over the word with him. He knew it. Bankim took his time: he asked for the definition, the origin, and the use of it in a sentence. And then he took a step toward the mike and spelled it correctly. The judge announced the next word: *auteur*. Bankim asked for the definition, kept his head down for about ten seconds, and then spelled the word out correctly.

The applause was long and loud. Arun squeezed Uma's pinky, and the two of them stood there for a few seconds. The boys had won competitions before. But this one felt different, like she'd won as well. They walked up to the stage, where the judges and the other participants were congratulating Bankim. The family waited for a few minutes, but when the crowd didn't appear to be thinning, they walked through it. Pankaj slapped Bankim's arm, Arun gave him an awkward hug, and Uma fixed his hair.

They'd been through the aftermath before with Pankaj. Then, it was simply one boy, one victory. This time there were more story angles for the newspapers: Bankim's victory, his perseverance, the brothers' joint victory. Uma filled out the proper paperwork, and they stood onstage taking pictures and answering questions from the local newspapers. Uma knew that though the newspapers were only small, stories had the ability to grow bigger with every retelling. She placed most of her hope in the local TV station. If they were there from the beginning, surely they'd captured Bankim's fall and rise. She couldn't wait to see how it looked on film.

The TV reporter asked Uma if he could interview Bankim.

"Of course," she said.

"Do you want your mom to be with you?" the reporter asked.

Without looking at her, he said, "No, I'll be fine."

The reporter asked Bankim how he felt after the fall.

"When I was standing up there for my—what round was it?"

"I think it was the third," the reporter said.

"Right. When I was standing up there for my third word, I felt very dizzy and disoriented. I went blank for a few seconds. That's when I must have fallen. But the second I fell and hit the ground, I felt better. I didn't feel great, but I really wanted to keep going."

Uma thought he'd freeze up in front of the camera, but he was perfectly comfortable. Uma and Bankim had not made eye contact since she had gotten up onstage. She assumed he was overwhelmed and busy.

After Bankim finished with the reporters, the crowd began to disperse. Uma and Arun thanked the judges, and the four of them headed back to the car. In the parking lot, Pankaj and Arun were walking ahead, while Uma and Bankim followed about twenty yards behind. She was happy finally to have a word. She wanted to congratulate him for his masterful performance. It was just like they'd planned, but even better. They'd decided that the third word would be the best moment to fall. At that point, there would still be enough participants and audience members to get the best effect. Uma had been thinking about the plan for several months. Spelling bees had some suspense, but they were never exciting. If there was going to be any excitement, something extraordinary needed to happen. Unfortunately, it wasn't going to grow naturally out of the competition. The idea of Bankim falling had just come to her. Even if he didn't win, he'd be the one people would remember and even cheer for. For months, she had kept the idea to herself. But the longer she thought about it, the more she felt like it was a reasonable plan. A month before the bee, she had talked to Bankim. She thought he'd tell her she was crazy. But he reacted with neither excitement nor disbelief. He treated it like it was a reasonable request, as if she'd asked him to wear his brown pants instead of the blue ones. And so they practiced, after school before Arun and Pankaj got home. Falls to the left, falls to the right. She taught him to use his hands to break the fall. She made him promise not to tell anybody.

And when he finally did it earlier that morning, it was better than any of the practice rounds. He used his hands without any hesitation. Uma wanted to know what he had been thinking while he was up there, and she wanted to know how he did that thing with his eyes. They'd not practiced that. They could talk about all this at home; for now she simply wanted to congratulate him. But right when she turned to him, Bankim looked straight ahead and picked up his step toward Arun and Pankaj.

The second he took that step away from her, she knew he was gone. She knew, because mothers can sense these things about their children. Somewhere between their initial conversation and now, Bankim decided that his mother had asked him to do something mothers shouldn't ask of their children. Uma thought she could catch up with him, and so she picked up her speed. The closer she got to him, the closer he got to Arun and Pankaj. By the time she'd made some ground, Bankim was walking between his brother and father. As she saw Arun put his arm around him, she stopped and labored to catch her breath. She felt a tiny, sharp prick behind her right eye, the beginning of a headache she'd been fighting off all morning. There was the boy she loved and craved more than anything else. She kept repeating in her mind that she'd done it for his sake, because if she didn't convince herself of this, she'd fall right down in that parking lot.

When she reached the car, they were already in their seats.

"Bankim, you choose where we're going to eat," Arun said. "We're celebrating."

"It doesn't matter," Bankim said.

"Of course it matters," Arun said.

Bankim didn't respond. Arun looked at Uma, asking her to say something.

"C'mon sweetie," Uma said, turning her head to face him. Someone needed to fill the silence. "Pick something."

And perhaps because of the look in her eyes or the way the word "sweetie" rolled off her tongue, Bankim started crying. Pankaj looked at him, and Arun watched him through the rearview mirror, but neither said anything. Uma reached back and placed her hand on his knee. He didn't move it away. There was no way for her to recover that part of Bankim she'd ushered away. But she still had that part of him that could break down in the moment when his own confusion about adult life crossed paths with her sweet voice. In that moment, he was still all hers.

"He wants pizza," Uma said and nudged Arun to start driving.

Ajay the Lover

That summer, the first woman he met had spent the previous three years on tour with Cirque du Soleil performing a piece inspired by her training in classical Indian dance. Neela had recently left the Cirque. She was tired of touring and was now applying to law school. She had been in the Bay Area visiting some friends, and leading up to their date, all Ajay could think about was her perfect dancer's body. The thought aroused him, but only until he remembered his own, which had never been in ideal shape. He had grown into a tall, well-built man, but he had been a chubby kid and could never quite get rid of the little rolls on his belly, no matter how hard he tried. And in pictures, he thought his face looked fat. At dinner, she took off her jacket; she was wearing a tight, black tee-shirt that showed her flat stomach. She was taller than he had expected. They met for Italian food, and they talked through the courses. She ate well and drank half a bottle of wine. But he fixated early on the hoop through her right nostril. While he could love a good nose ring, on her it was unattractive.

"Conversation was good," Ajay said.
"And?"
"And, well, it made her look like a dyke."
"I thought you liked nose rings." Vikram was Ajay's oldest, most patient friend, and they had talked extensively about the things Ajay liked.

19

"I do, but it's the first thing my mother will notice. She will take me to the side and ask me why I have brought *that* home."

"You can ask her to take it off."

"And she lives in New York. When am I ever going to move to New York?"

A pattern had emerged over the course of Ajay's twenties. He'd go out with a woman, and around the one-month mark, he'd decide on their long-term potential. He said he needed one month to determine if there was enough passion and mutual understanding to carry them into a relationship. He thought he had an effective formula, but he remained unmarried as the rest of his friends paired off. Every once in a while, his parents asked whether he had any prospects.

When he passed thirty, the expectation that Ajay should get married sooner rather than later became more explicit. His parents never came out and said it, though his mother did begin to offer to set him up with the daughters of various friends. His parents had been married for more years than he realized, his older brother was married, and most of his cousins were either married, close to marrying, or in the closet. He'd noticed that his father treated his brother more as an adult after he got married. And as long as Ajay stayed single, he remained a student or, at best, a young man. For his family, marriage, more than a good job and home ownership, marked the beginning of manhood.

He sent word out that he needed help. He requested introductions. Among his friends, there was a growing competition about who could best set Ajay up. Most of them didn't really believe they had the perfect woman, but a competitive spirit had spread, and everyone lobbied for their candidate. Vikram didn't know any single women, at least any that would interest Ajay. He just wanted his friend to be married.

One night Ajay went to a club to meet a friend of a friend. The woman he was meeting brought along her older sister, who had come because she wanted to see the club scene. At one point in the night, away from the noise of the bar and the dance floor, Ajay sat in a booth with the two sisters. The younger sister was nice, but they had little to say to each other. Perhaps there would have been better opportunity to talk if the older sister had not been there. But she was, and she and Ajay did most of the talking. She had come to see the club but seemed impatient with the loud music and the drunkenness of carefree twenty-five-year-olds.

She was in her early thirties and worked as an architect. Ajay had always wanted to be an architect. It seemed to him the perfect blend of art and practicality. He knew a little about the stars—Gehry, Meier, Eisenman, Foster.

"You know that Tadao Ando is finally building in America," he said.

"Yeah," she replied. "In Fort Worth. It's a step up for Texas." She didn't show any surprise that he knew something about her world. Ajay thought that she should have been delighted. How many guys did she meet in bars who asked her about Tadao Ando?

Soon, the younger sister slipped away, and he ordered them beers.

At first, neither of them said very much. He was there, after all, to meet her sister. But then a song came on that sampled a beat that they could not place.

"Rick Springfield?"

"No," she said. But she did smile.

They tried to remember the original song, and then they talked about the music they liked. She said she had been listening to a lot of Neil Young lately. The more she talked, the more comfortable and expressive she became. Her teeth seemed perfect to him. She was the type of woman who never got cavities. They talked about movies and travel—easy topics for a first meeting. They had traveled around Spain and Portugal the same summer. She said how much she disliked romantic comedies. He would have agreed either way, though he disliked them as well.

He asked about her job.

"I worked at a large firm for several years with bad pay and a lot of apprentice work. But for the past year, I've been working for a smaller firm where I have a lot more responsibility. We also do a lot of public projects. I was getting a little tired of designing people's homes."

"Can you at least do my house?"

"You can't afford me," she said and took the last sip of her beer.

They talked about the different architects she liked as they had another drink.

"Why are you so interested in all this?" she asked.

"I can't draw a straight line, so it's nice to talk about people who can."

Later they moved to the dance floor, and at one point, he was dancing with both sisters. He had his fantasies.

At the end of the night, the elder sister gave him her card: Sara Khalid.

"She's smart, we had a fantastic conversation, and we have a lot of the same tastes. But it can't work."

"Why?" Vikram asked.

"Her family is from Islamabad. It would be fine for six months. But it can't work in the long run."

"Does she practice?"

"I don't think so, but even so. You know I can't be with a Muslim. It doesn't feel right."

"But she doesn't practice. You're not a practicing Hindu."

"But it's in the soul. She has a Muslim soul." Ajay knew that this made no logical sense, but Vikram provided him the space to be illogical, to feel and not to think.

"Any other problems?"

"She's too old and knowing. I don't want anyone my age."

In a booklet sent to all members of their subcaste, in India and abroad, Ajay's parents wrote down his profile: five eleven, fair complexion, BA and MBA. His mother called him at work one afternoon and said this one could not be missed. He had resisted setups by his parents before, but now, doubting his ability to find a woman on his own, he did not object. Madhuri was visiting California with her parents, and they contacted Ajay's parents after seeing his name in the booklet. She works in the movies, said his mother. He did not trust her ability to read between the lines. "Works in the movies" could have easily meant that she was an assistant on the set or a script copier. When they met, he was glad he had allowed his mother to meddle. Madhuri was a knockout in the way that rich women from Bombay are knockouts: she had red lips, unblemished skin—quite a feat considering she lived in the tropics—and a fashion sense that was some mix of Bombay and LA. She was wearing a cap with the bill off center. They met at a nice Chinese restaurant. She came with her older sister and her brother-in-law.

He had taken to watching Hindi movies lately. She looked familiar and could easily have been one of the stars in the films. Her name—Madhuri Bhatt—was very filmy. But if she was one of those stars, why was she looking for a husband in California? Bombay had plenty of handsome men who were rich, worked out, and wore earrings.

Once again, Ajay found himself talking to the other sister. Madhuri was shielded away and only spoke to her sister, and occasionally to her brother-in-law, and they conveyed her answers to Ajay.

Ajay began by asking about her involvement in the movies.

The sister answered, "Madhuri has been in a couple of small films, but there is a big one coming up. She starts shooting in September."

"How exciting," Ajay said. "What movies were you in?"

Madhuri whispered in her sister's ear. "Madhuri's disappointed that you don't know."

"I'm sorry, but work has kept me really busy." He tried again: "What movie are you going to be in?"

"She can't talk about that. It's part of her contract. But it's going to be big."

Ajay gave up trying to ask Madhuri questions and started talking directly to the sister and the brother-in-law. She wrote for a movie magazine and he was a banker, and they both lived in Bombay. Ajay and the brother-in-law talked about their jobs. He asked Ajay about management consulting because consulting opportunities were growing in Bombay and he wanted to move away from banking.

Finally, Madhuri asked a question. "Ask him," she began, "whether he's interested in living in Bombay."

He knew the answer she wanted, and he didn't want to give it. She didn't seem so pretty anymore. Of course, he liked the prospect of marrying a Bollywood film actress. What young Indian man didn't? But he couldn't get past the absurdity of this exchange. Was the process of only speaking to each other through intermediaries supposed to be coy, a method of creating interest? "I could see myself having a flat there and spending three or four weeks a year and maybe a full winter now and then when I get the time, but nothing permanent."

He assumed that eventually he'd find somebody, but as he was driving home from his meeting with Madhuri, he began to question that assumption. His life was a farce.

At a party one Friday night, he started talking to Priya, a woman he had seen at various parties over the past year. She was part of his large circle of friends and acquaintances. When they finally talked, there was some spark, though she seemed more interested than he was. He knew she had asked a common friend of theirs about him. But as the night wore on, his interest grew. They slept together that night, but he didn't call her for several days after. They met again the next Saturday night, had dinner, and spent another night together. In a bout of honesty the following morning, Ajay told her that he wasn't interested in a relationship. "Don't worry," she said. "Neither am I."

"Did you spend the night again?" Vikram asked.

"Shut up."

"You did."

"Shut up," Ajay said again. Though he'd enjoyed his evenings with Priya, he felt quite a bit of shame that their meetings were based on simple desire. He saw her several more times, but he didn't tell Vikram.

At work, an attractive woman named Rachel joined his group. He didn't know that Rachel was Jewish until she told him.

"We're nominally Jewish."

"Nominally?" Ajay was well educated. He went to Berkeley and prided himself on reading widely, from the *New York Times* and the *Wall Street Journal* to biographies and histories. He loved to demonstrate his knowledge, but his intelligence could be dull at times. It was hard for him to handle nuance.

"I'm not religious, and neither are my parents. No Sabbath for us. We're just Jews."

He knew about the Sabbath, but he didn't know its exact significance for Jews. He didn't ask.

They had this conversation in the first month they knew each other.

And in the months that followed, he talked her through a breakup with her boyfriend of two years. She said she was convinced all along that he was the right person, and then one day, after he had been away for a week on a hiking trip with his college friends, he came back and said it was over. He said he was uncertain about her.

Rachel stopped eating and began to lose weight. Ajay started bringing her little snacks—a muffin in the morning, biscotti in the afternoon. He insisted they eat lunch together, and he made sure that she ate. They never talked about the fact that she was not eating. She was the slow crush that he'd not had as an adult. He found himself thinking about her in the evenings. A couple of mornings a week, he was excited to figure out what breakfast sweet to bring her.

And then one morning, he brought her hash browns from McDonald's. While he was getting them, it seemed like a fun idea. But as he was walking towards her desk with the bag in his hands, he felt he had made a mistake. He opened the bag and saw that the little bag they had placed the hash brown in was soaked with grease. He was going to throw it away, but he wanted an excuse to see Rachel. She always looked perfect first thing in the morning in her well-pressed suits.

"It looked much better at McDonald's than it does now," Ajay said as he placed the bag on her desk.

She opened up the bag and looked inside.

"You really don't have to eat it."

She took it out and had a bite. They chatted for a few minutes about a project they'd both worked on. "Are you traveling this week?" she asked. Management consulting required a lot of travel.

"Phoenix. Are you?"

"Tucson," she said.

She finished the hash browns, carefully wiped around her mouth with a napkin so that she wouldn't smudge her lipstick, and slowly folded the bag several times before throwing it away.

"Have you ever been to the Grand Canyon?" she asked.

"Once with my family a long time ago. I think I was ten."

"I don't know how far it is, but maybe I'll stop by after I'm done with Tucson. I'd like to see it."

She left him an opening that he had been waiting for, and now with it in front of him, he couldn't move forward. He was scared of her. They were the same age, they liked the same kind of movies, they were both the middle of three children; they even looked alike in the way that Semites and Indians can look alike. And there was plenty of attraction. But he was scared because they were ideal for each other and because he had a good feeling about their long-term possibility.

"Yes," he said. "You should check out the Grand Canyon. It's a really nice place." They talked about her client in Tucson, and then he walked out of her office.

Vikram wanted to meet Rachel.

"They don't marry outside their group. What's the use of starting something if it isn't going to go anywhere?"

Vikram asked what it mattered if it went nowhere. There would be some fun, and wasn't that enough? Ajay said that it wasn't. Vikram thought that if they started small, they could build up to something bigger.

"Has she said she won't marry a non-Jew?"

"She doesn't need to say it. I know."

Vikram had found love easily. He and his wife often talked about how they fell in love. Being Indian helped initially—they had similar pressures from their parents, they took an Indian history class together. But they thought they fell in love because they experienced the intensity of college together. And Vikram remembered some friends of his parents who boasted, "Ours was a *love* marriage. Nothing was arranged for us." Vikram had reached that ideal. His wife just happened to be Indian. He couldn't understand Ajay's insistence on being able to love only an Indian woman.

"You experience the same intensity because you are both Indian," Ajay said.

"It helped, but it wasn't everything."

They were at Ajay's place, having a few drinks.

"It's in the soul. You only fall in love with a woman whose soul is like yours. You can only feel intimate if she breathes the world in the same way you do. I can't explain it. There is a core that brings you together, and language and the place you come from creates that core. Talking in Gujarati gives me an intimacy that I can't have in English."

"Your Gujarati is horrible."

"It's not that bad," Ajay responded quickly and then continued: "Knowing that we come from the same place matters. She has to have an Indian, Hindu soul. Rachel and I look like we can get along, but we can't. The essence is not the same. I know this sounds silly, but it's the way things work."

"Ajay, you're drunk."

"No," he pleaded. "I'm serious. There are a lot of mixed marriages, but most people stay close to themselves when they get married. I just want to be like most people."

Until recently, Ajay hadn't questioned his parents' decision to move to America, partly because they'd never questioned it. But now that he was an adult, responsible for his own happiness, he had been thinking about the move. From how his parents described it, and from the little memory he had, they had had a pretty good life there. He tried to imagine the details of his alternate life had they remained in India. In a country with a relatively high level of poverty, his family's upper-middle-class status would have given them a good life—a large apartment in central Bombay, help around the house, a driver. And he'd been rethinking the possibility of an arranged marriage. For years, he thought such arrangements were old-fashioned and unromantic. The men who willingly entered such marriages were wimps, unable to create their own social lives. Now thinking of them simply as introductions, the whole thing didn't seem so bad. "If we'd stayed, my parents would have found a perfect match for me, letting the planets do the work. No running around, no searching in bars."

"That's right," Vikram said. "That recent introduction went so well."

Ajay believed in the importance of being with a particular type of Indian woman and that he'd find the right one. But at that moment, it was hard to push away the confusion the search had created. Perhaps he would not find the woman he was meant to marry. Perhaps he would never get married. He hadn't really worked through these thoughts fully because they scared him. And to defend against going too far down this path, he took another sip of his drink and said, "It would have been easier for us if our parents stayed in India. America has fucked us."

Ajay looked at Vikram, with his goatee, his well-fitting jeans, and his beautiful Indian bride. Vikram caught Ajay looking at him.

"What?"

"You know you're lucky."

"With what?"

"You're in a solid relationship. It must help you deal with anything that goes wrong. Bad day at work but warm body at home."

"It's nice," said Vikram. "It doesn't solve all my problems, but it makes life easier. My parents are comfortable with the situation, and so are Sejal's. It's comfort all around."

The summer ended. For the next two months, Ajay saw nobody. Partly he was sick of going on dates, but mainly he had already met or gone out with most of the women his friends knew. Now nobody was calling. There had been rain, cold rain, and now it was quiet. But then, as the holidays were nearing, he made another effort.

Ajay was apprehensive about many things in his life. He didn't do things that he thought weren't in his best interest. But there was adventurousness in him, and he would try anything once. Vikram had told him about speed dating. Indian speed dating.

Ajay paid his thirty-dollar reservation fee and learned that the event would be held in a Pacific Heights bar. How it worked became clearer once he arrived. There were fifteen men and fifteen women all between the ages of twenty-five and thirty-five. He walked in and talked to the "host," who gave him a scorecard and a badge with a number. There were fifteen tables for two set up. These were the rules: he would spend three minutes talking to the woman across the table from him, and then a whistle would blow and he would move on to the next table and talk to the next woman. After each conversation, he would circle *Yes* or *No* next to the number assigned to the woman he had been talking to. The host insisted that the circling be done discreetly. At the end, the host would collect the cards, marking the end of the evening. The next day, they would tabulate the scorecards, and each man and woman who had met and talked, and who both circled *Yes,* would receive each other's email address.

The bar had a nice vibe—Nusrat on the stereo, generous bar drinks, and the lights dim enough to see the person across the table clearly but not bright enough to scope out everyone in the bar. Though Ajay recognized the irony, he thought all of the men were there because they were socially inept. He didn't want to talk to any of them, and no one made an attempt to talk to him before the event started. At eight p.m. sharp, the speed dating began.

The first woman, Mala, was a South Indian doctor. A pediatrician. He wanted her to be a heart surgeon or a surgeon of any type. He wondered whether she wore clogs. He found doctors in clogs very sexy. They talked about her practice, and as with other doctors he knew, that was all they talked about. Then the whistle blew, and Ajay circled *No.*

The next woman was getting over a divorce; she was not yet thirty. "You need to know sooner or later, and what's the use of knowing later? It's a waste of time for both of us." Ajay liked her, and he liked her unusual green eyes, but he didn't like her divorce. Whistle and *No.*

Bela was next. She was a corporate lawyer who looked like she made a lot of money. He noticed her Cartier and her nice black suit—she said she had come straight from work. She was born in South Africa but had lived most of her life in California. She was beautiful. He wondered why she needed to come to such an event. They talked about the law, and Ajay knew that he was going to circle *Yes*. And for the first time that night, he began looking around to get a sense of his competition. The whistle blew, and he moved on.

The next one made his heart sink. It was the architect, Sara, whom he had not called. He sat down, and they both started laughing. Ajay laughed partly because of the circumstance of their second meeting and partly out of the guilt of not having called her. She laughed with her whole face. Right then, he felt very attracted to her. She had not laughed like that at the club. He asked her how her work was going. She told him she was working on a project to design an elementary school. Her firm was figuring out ways to make the classrooms and the play areas feel connected to one another. They were going to use steel beams and glass to make the school seem airy and light. That night at the club, Ajay had loved the way she talked about her work. And he loved the way she talked about it now. He wanted to ask her so many questions. Of the many first meetings he had with women that summer, his conversation with Sara had the greatest ease.

There was a second of silence after she was done talking about the school. "I was looking forward to your phone call," she said.

He gave himself a couple of seconds. There was an easy way out of this. "I just didn't think it would work."

She moved her right hand back and forth between them, as if to draw a line in the air. "What about this can't work? I am laughing and talking to you about my job. They are the two things I like most."

Ajay had no response, at least none that he could say to her. The whistle blew. "I am sorry," he said as he got up from the table. He felt sad but resolute in his turn away from her. *No.*

The next six women were unmemorable, or memorable for the wrong reasons. One had a mole right below her left nostril, another had yellow teeth. He realized that most of the women attending these events were not very attractive. He thought that this was one place where he was allowed to be completely shallow. This was, after all, a completely superficial event—in three minutes, all you had to go on was some physical chemistry, and then maybe, if you were lucky, one person said something that struck you as being interesting.

As he was going through the list of women, he felt a little bit of a panic. He had spoken with ten, and he had circled *Yes* for only one of them, and she was the prettiest of them all. All the other guys would pick her as well. He didn't really care, but he wanted some dates out of this event. He needed a bit of a boost to his ego. The panic continued until he got to the first of the last three women.

Her name was Stacey. It was an initial turnoff—either she had changed her name or she had the type of parents who would give an Indian girl a name like Stacey. But she improved. She was close to being done with her doctorate in biochemistry. "I want to make a lot of money working for a pharmaceutical company." Ajay laughed. "I'm serious," she said. He appreciated a woman that spoke freely about money. Whistle and *Yes*.

The next was Uma. She was short and nice enough, and by the time Ajay had made it to her table, she was completely sloshed. She said she had had two glasses of wine to numb her nervousness, and it was two glasses more than she regularly drank. She started making fun of some of the guys she met that night. She did not whisper. Ajay liked this spirit. The other women were so careful about how they came off. Whistle and *Yes*.

And finally there was Kavita. There had to be at least one Kavita in the room because one didn't have to go far to find Indian parents who thought their child was a *poem*. She was pretty—thick black hair, high cheek bones, long, thin fingers.

"Nice cuff links," she said when he sat down.

He tugged at the ends of his sleeves. "Thank you." She was the first person that night to give him a compliment. She moved forward and looked at them closely. They had several different shades of blue stones set against a silver back.

"You'll have to let me borrow them sometime," she said. Whistle and *Yes*.

Then Ajay turned in his scorecard and fled the bar.

For their first date, Kavita insisted they meet during the day. Was he somebody who looked threatening to women? But by the second date, she was ready for the evening. For their third date, they went to see the extended version of *Apocalypse Now* that had just come out. Kavita had never heard of the movie, but she said she was willing to see anything. He suggested it because he wanted to see something a little artsy. He knew that artsy could be pretentious, but he wanted to impress Kavita.

As they were waiting in line at the food counter, Kavita asked, "What is the movie about again?"

"Vietnam."

"What goes with a war movie?"

"What goes?"

"In terms of food."

This seemed an absolutely absurd thing to ask, but it made Ajay want to go into the movie theater and start making out with her the second the lights went out.

Ajay looked at the options but could not come up with anything. "Nachos?" Kavita asked.

"No. No serious food. Candy might be better."

"Candy it is," she said. When they got to the counter, she ordered Twizzlers and Skittles, and she asked Ajay to get some popcorn for himself in case she got a little hungry.

In the middle of the movie, after a particularly tense scene when Chef and Willard go looking for mangoes in the jungle, Ajay and Kavita looked at each other and Kavita maintained eye contact for a second longer than necessary. Ajay went in to kiss her, but Kavita said, "Shh. Later."

But by the end of the movie, neither was in the mood for kissing.

"Wow," Kavita said. "That was a horrible date movie."

"I'm sorry."

"It's fine," she said. "I really liked it."

They went for a drink after, and they spent some time talking about the movie. Mostly they talked about Marlon Brando. "Did you see his hands?" she asked.

Ajay had not noticed them.

"They were enormous. He could crush a baby's head with them."

Ajay didn't know how to respond.

"I mean that in this character, you could see how his hands make him seem so monstrous."

"Have you seen him lately? He's become really fat. He can barely move, and he breathes real heavy."

"Yes," she said. "He reminds me of Shashi Kapoor."

That may have been the moment when he first began to be seriously interested in her. Shashi Kapoor was an icon of Bollywood film in the '70s and '80s and was, like Brando, very handsome as a young man. But in his later years, he gained a lot of weight. Ajay had made the comparison once himself and was quite proud of it.

"I've been meaning to ask you something," she began as they were leaving the bar. "How many names did you get in your email?"

Ajay was embarrassed and thought about inflating the number. "One," he said. "You were the only one."

"How many *Yes*es did you circle?"

"Four."

"One out of four? That's dismal, Ajay."

"How about you?" he asked.

"I got four names, but I circled the other three before I got to you. I wouldn't have circled *Yes* for the others if I had seen you first." She turned away as she said this, seeming surprisingly shy.

At the end of the night, it was Kavita who pulled Ajay to her and kissed him. Between kisses, she said, "If you wanted to get in my pants, you should have taken me to a comedy. That movie is going to set me back for days."

They were together for four months, and he thought he had finally found the right woman. She was perfect in many ways: a high-caste Hindu, a few years younger than he was, a beautiful haiku. Her Gujarati was better than his. They went dancing together and played tennis on the weekends. It didn't bother him much that she was a better tennis player. He felt justified in his insistence on waiting all this time for the right woman. He even gloated a little in front of Vikram.

But then Ajay got restless and a little tired. There was something overwhelming about her directness and her quirkiness. She was direct about what she wanted for dinner ("I hate sushi"), and she was direct in bed ("That smells a little"). At parties, she chatted with everyone. Ajay would still be hanging up their coats while she was already in the middle of a conversation, halfway through a beer. And then there was the drinking. She was a drinker—lots of whatever was available. If she started with beer, she ended with it. And if she started with martinis, well, she would end with martinis in the bathroom, over the toilet. Kavita was the type of woman he knew in college—they were on the intramural soccer team, and they could drink with you. But you couldn't go out with them. They were buddies. And Kavita had become a buddy, a beautiful buddy, but a buddy nonetheless.

He was a little scared of talking to her directly, so he wrote her a letter. He convinced himself that writing the letter was the better, classier way of ending their relationship. It would give him the opportunity to articulate his feelings fully. He wrote that he was confused, uncertain about the direction of their relationship, and thought it was best they spend time apart. It was not an easy letter to write. He had really grown to like her, but he couldn't deal with her high energy.

Two nights later, she came over unannounced. He had been expecting her. "This is bullshit, Ajay. What the hell are you saying? This letter says nothing. I like to be up-front about things, and I think I deserve at least that from you."

Ajay tried to restate what he had written in the letter, but she stood there unconvinced. She had the power, somehow, to know when he was saying the truth and when he wasn't. The only thing that would satisfy her was the truth.

"OK, Kavita. You're not the type of person I want."

"Good," she said. "What type of person am I?"

"You come on, well, you come on kind of strong."

"What does that mean? Please just say what you want."

"Kavita, you're a little too . . . I am looking for someone a little softer."

"Softer?"

Ajay knew he shouldn't have said it, but she had been pushing him harder and harder. "Someone a little more feminine."

He was done. Her face no longer demanded answers. Ajay moved closer to her because he thought she would want a hug or something. But as he got closer, she popped him just below his right eye. It came quickly and ended quickly. It took him several seconds to realize what had happened.

"You fat pig," she said and then turned around and walked toward the front door. He stood dazed for a few seconds. He didn't know whether to be angry at Kavita for hitting him or at himself for being so insensitive. She insisted on the truth, and he had been honest. He was not to blame.

"Kavita, please wait." As much as he liked the feeling of being a rogue right then, he thought it was not who he was. He wished he could just let her walk out the door. But they had had too nice of a thing together to end on such an abrupt note. "Please wait one minute."

She turned around and waited by the front door.

"I didn't mean it like that," Ajay began. "It's just that you and I are a little too different."

"My parents are different from each other, but they've been together for thirty years."

Kavita said this to show Ajay that difference was not the deal breaker, but all he heard was thirty years. "That's a long time."

"How long have your parents been together?"

35

"I don't know, but somewhere around there. Thirty-five I think." It was hard for him to imagine that long of a period with another person.

They were silent for a moment. He had told her to wait to make himself feel better, but he had nothing to say.

Before Kavita turned to leave, she said, "I really don't care that you think I'm not feminine enough. But it's fucked up. You're fucked up."

Vikram came over a few nights later.

"What the hell happened?"

"Nothing."

As he told Vikram the story, he kept touching around his right eye, encircling the sore area. It had turned an ugly shade of black and blue and gray. Finally, he placed his finger on the bone right below the eye, harder than he intended. He felt a sharp pain. And perhaps because of that pain, Ajay started crying.

"This is not what I was promised," Ajay said.

"What exactly were you promised?" Vikram asked.

Ajay thought for a few seconds: "An end to this looking."

"You can end it the second you want. But you won't because you like it too much." There was a sharpness in Vikram's voice that hadn't been there before. The phrase fell out of his mouth like he'd prepared it beforehand.

"What do I like so much?"

"You know. The whole drama of looking around and the disappointment. You don't really want anybody. You just like the process of wanting." Vikram paused and then continued. "Things might be a little easier if you just realized this."

Ajay went to the bathroom to blow his nose and thought about what Vikram had said. He stayed there longer than he needed, trying to work through the various explanations for his continued failure. Perhaps he hadn't allowed himself to practice being in a long-term relationship. Or he hadn't met the right woman. Maybe it was something deeper that he was a little scared to consider. But he could come up with no clear understanding of his situation.

When he came out of the bathroom, Ajay asked, "If the lecture is over, can we go get a drink?"

They went to a place near Ajay's apartment and sat down at the bar. Vikram's wife, Sejal, was going to meet them there later. A woman, tall and attractive with dark blond hair, was tending bar that night. They recognized each other from the times Ajay had come in on his own, but they had never gotten past small talk while she was making his drink.

"Hey," she said and placed two napkins in front of them.

Vikram ordered a beer, and Ajay ordered a scotch.

She got them their drinks. But instead of going back to the other side of the bar, she stood near them and turned her head to the TV. She had never lingered like this before. The Giants game was on.

"Do you guys watch baseball?"

"Sure," Ajay said.

They talked about Barry Bonds and the prospects for the team. It was early in the season. She introduced herself and offered her hand. "My name is Eileen." They watched the game for few minutes until she was called away by someone at the other end of the bar.

Ajay leaned over to Vikram and whispered, "Women like injured men."

Ajay watched her as she prepared drinks and leaned down to remove a few bottles of beer from the fridge. Of course, she wasn't his type. But that didn't matter right then. He liked the nervousness he felt around his shoulders, and he liked the challenge of figuring out what he would say to her next. *Come on back,* he said to himself. *Come on back here.* And every time she seemed to be coming his way, Ajay could feel his chest constrict.

"Maybe you're right," he said to Vikram.

Vikram took a sip of his beer, smiled, but didn't say anything.

"I really tried with Kavita, but I just couldn't do it." He heard his mother's insistent inquiries, getting less gentle as he grew older. And he heard his father say without much irony, "Please, please don't let me die with you still unsettled." He pictured the many weddings he'd attended in the past several years. He was so tired of those voices and images. He was tired of the expectation he'd placed on himself. "I can't produce the intimacy she demanded. And I don't have the patience to work through all the problems, every day."

"That's fine," Vikram said. "Some people aren't meant to be in a relationship. I function better in one, and you function better without one." Vikram held up his glass to toast Ajay. "Here's to uncertainty."

Ajay took a long sip of his drink and then another. He wondered what happened to men like him. He couldn't get Kavita out of his mind.

He got up and went to the bathroom. When he came out, he saw Sejal enter the bar. He stood back and watched them. She had a big smile on her face, as if it had been much longer than that morning since she'd seen her husband. Vikram got up and kissed her cheek. They fell into some conversation, and they both looked like they were genuinely interested in what the other was saying. Ajay had always envied the ease between them. He continued to watch as Eileen went over, took Sejal's order, and grabbed a bottle of beer from the fridge. And then she went and stood at the far end of the bar from Vikram and Sejal.

This wasn't about Ajay's inability to commit or to love. And it wasn't about him being a bit of a cad, though he liked the idea that someone might think that of him. This was about being selfish and feeling that it wasn't such a bad thing. He felt free. And a little frightened of what lay ahead.

Ajay walked up to Eileen, ordered another drink, and as she was preparing it, asked, "Do you know anything about cricket? It's a much better game than baseball."

Welcome Back, Mahesh

After spending eighteen months in a minimum-security prison for grand theft, Mahesh Shah could not clearly picture the new life he wanted. He looked forward to seeing his family but wanted a couple of weeks by himself, away from prison and his old life. While he had spent a great deal of his sentence working in the prison library, and becoming the prison Scrabble champion, each member of his immediate family had developed different ideas about the Mahesh who had sold hundreds of bottles of stolen vodka at the family liquor store and the Mahesh who was now returning after paying the price for his yearlong moment of weakness.

Mahesh's father grew up hearing about how Gandhi and Nehru read, wrote, and planned the Indian independence movement from prison. Prison was a heroic place, a place you chose to go to, a place where you sacrificed the ease of your own life for the sake of a larger purpose, a place of gathering before the battle. His father's uncle spent time in a British jail during the independence movement. And though that uncle presumably had more altruistic reasons for placing himself in harm's way, his life after he got out became one moment of success after another. His prison time was a badge of his masculinity, his allegiance to good, righteous causes, and his willingness to sacrifice. He became a very wealthy merchant and married a beautiful woman above his physical league and social standing. Prison was the best thing that had happened to him. Mahesh's time in prison, on the other hand, would not be remembered in the same manner.

Mahesh's younger brother, Nikhil, was far from disappointed. Over the past several years, he'd gone through different phases in relation to his family. Because of his intelligence and good looks, he was part of a smart, wealthy clique in high school. He used to be embarrassed about his parents owning a gas station and a liquor store, while his friends' parents were doctors and engineers. But he came back to the family after the restaurant they started became successful. There were write-ups in the *San Francisco Chronicle* and in guidebooks: "Sharmila Shah cooks her native Gujarati cuisine with great care and a steady hand. It is well worth the drive from San Francisco." And the liquor store was doing better than ever since they started selling fine, expensive wine. Nikhil liked the idea of his parents being successful restaurateurs, and he liked the money they were amassing after years of working hard. Later, after taking a class on the sociology of wealth in America during the second semester of his freshman year at Berkeley, he began to think of his family as working-class merchants slowly working their way up and Mahesh's time in jail as a working-class event. Mahesh was a victim of the pressures inflicted on the workingman.

Mahesh's mother visited her son only once in prison. They opened the restaurant soon after he went to jail, and though his troubles postponed the opening, they eventually helped the place do well. She worked in that restaurant every hour she could, first in buying furniture and prints for the walls, then in setting up the menu, and finally in cooking every night. She kept Mahesh out of her mind by concentrating on *Sharmila's*.

The day Mahesh was released, his father and brother were waiting for him in the parking lot in a brand-new, cream-colored Cadillac Seville. His father was in the driver's seat, and Nikhil sat in the back. Since Mahesh and Nikhil had been young, they had fought over the front seat, and even when they grew old enough to know better, there was always a silent race to get shotgun.

Mahesh opened the passenger-side door, sat down, and carefully placed his blue Adidas duffle bag at his feet. The leather seats were large and soft; the car had a luxury he'd forgotten. The engine was running, but he couldn't hear it. He shook his father's hand and then turned and shook hands with Nikhil. Though they'd visited recently, he felt like it had been much longer. He was happy to be among familiar faces.

"It's beautiful," he said.

His father leaned forward and hit a button. Bhimsen Joshi, the Indian devotional singer, flooded the car. "Ten speakers," he said. He turned up the volume to demonstrate their power, kept it high for a few seconds longer than necessary, and then turned it down. "They were selling off last year's model. I picked it up last week." He paused for a few seconds: "This is the longest trip I've made."

Mahesh hadn't seen his father so excited in a long time.

As they drove away from the prison, they talked about the car—its power, the engine, the gas mileage, and the stereo. Mahesh wasn't interested in the technicalities, but it was easy conversation.

His father liked fancy stereos and nice cars, but he was neither an audiophile nor did he obsess over the finer points of automobile engineering. He had always wanted a Cadillac, and year after year, he'd go to the dealership and inspect the new models. Over the years, he learned quite a bit about the technical aspects of the Seville. But each year, he would find a new excuse to wait for next year's model. It became a joke among Mahesh, Nikhil, and their mother. When Mahesh saw the car, he was genuinely surprised.

His father was driving in the slow lane, a hint above fifty-five. Mahesh could feel himself getting agitated. He saw a Taco Bell sign in the distance, and he hadn't eaten that morning in anticipation of tostadas and chicken soft tacos for lunch.

He asked his father whether they could stop.

"There's a big lunch waiting for you."

"Great," he said. "I've been looking forward to Mom's food. How is she?" He was disappointed about the tostadas and worried about the lunch. Could they have invited the extended family? Confused about how to handle his return, it was not beyond his parents to plan a gathering.

"Fine. She's always busy at the restaurant. And Nikhil has finally declared a major. Chemical Engineering." The father was proud of Nikhil's success in school.

"He told me in his letter."

"Nikhil wrote you letters?" He looked at Nikhil through the rearview mirror.

"Just a couple," Mahesh said, downplaying the number.

There was silence in the car.

"How's school?" Mahesh asked.

The two brothers talked about school while their father concentrated on driving.

The father was occupied by the thought of his sons communicating without his knowledge. He understood the legal reasons for Mahesh's prison sentence, but he still couldn't understand why he'd done something illegal. He thought he'd adequately taught his sons the difference between right and wrong. The entire affair—his arrest, the deal, the jail visits—was beyond the father's sense of reality. In the absence of understanding, he had managed the situation on the outside as tightly as he could. He insisted that he and Nikhil drive up together for regular visits. The communication between his sons, however, was outside of his management. And now he envied the understanding that must have existed between them in those letters.

Nikhil told Mahesh about the classes he'd taken but rushed through the details to get to what Mahesh had to say. "Did you read them?" he asked.

Before Mahesh could answer, his father interjected: "Read what?"

"The books Nikhil sent me," Mahesh said.

"Did you read the biography of Abraham Lincoln?"

The father had read a Lincoln biography in his twenties and liked it very much. Like other men of his generation, he loved biographies and admired the men they memorialized: Marcus Aurelius, Lincoln, Nehru, Franklin Roosevelt, among others.

"No. But I read ones on Thomas Jefferson and Churchill."

Nikhil knew that prison was difficult for Mahesh, but at least he had time on his hands. Maybe if he read enough, Mahesh would understand his life in the way that Nikhil was beginning to understand it. He sent him all sorts of things: the autobiographies of Gandhi, Malcolm X, and Mandela, *The Great Gatsby, Crime and Punishment, The Grapes of Wrath*. Nikhil had always been a good reader. He got bored easily and needed books and movies to occupy his time. He wondered if later he'd look back at having sent Mahesh these books as overly enthusiastic, a bit of college-boy immaturity. But he couldn't resist. He was overwhelmed by his realization that Mahesh's time in jail was more than just a failure of personal judgment. It was a turning point in Mahesh's life. Nikhil felt that he himself wouldn't be the same after all this either.

Mahesh read them all, slowly and with some difficulty. He knew that Nikhil thought he was some type of victim, and he went along with it, not because Nikhil was right but because the two of them were communicating in a way they hadn't since Mahesh was ten and Nikhil was eight. Through junior high and high school, they were tracked differently, and they came to believe the tracking. Nikhil did better in school; he made better decisions and choices about where to expend his energy. This became clear to Mahesh while he was in jail. Nikhil was moving through college, while Mahesh's imagination failed to provide him some sense of what he could do after he got out. He decided that he was going to try to learn why Nikhil's life seemed so much more on track. And so he read the books.

"What was your favorite?" Nikhil asked. He'd written Mahesh quite a few letters, but the few Mahesh wrote in response thanked him for the books without ever mentioning what he thought of them. The letters didn't say much about Mahesh's state of mind. Nikhil thought that he would have written a different type of letter were he in Mahesh's position, letters that served as a record.

"I'm not sure," Mahesh said.

"Think about it," Nikhil persisted.

"Let Mahesh rest," the father said. "You can talk later." The father and Nikhil had had an argument before they left the house. The father wanted to go by himself so that he could have the initial time alone with Mahesh. But Nikhil insisted, and the father relented, on the condition that Nikhil sit quietly.

Mahesh was willing to talk to Nikhil about the books, but he'd do it when he felt like it and not when Nikhil asked. He was ready to develop a new relationship with Nikhil, but Nikhil's insistence reminded him of the brother he knew so well. His parents had indulged Nikhil all his life. He'd been given whatever he wanted, whenever he wanted it. In his letters, Nikhil wanted full access to Mahesh's experience, wanting to know how Mahesh was doing and what he was feeling. Was he going through a transformation? Was he angry? Did he know it was OK to be angry? But Mahesh didn't want to give Nikhil the opportunity to analyze his fluctuations. He'd closely guarded the movement in his thinking over the previous eighteen months.

Nikhil leaned forward and asked in a hushed voice, "Did you bring the books back with you?" Mahesh turned his head to look back at Nikhil without moving the rest of his body. Nikhil saw the expression on only half his face when he said, "No, I left them back in the prison library." The expression Nikhil saw was one of annoyance and impatience. Nikhil sat back in his seat, disappointed, and perhaps more dangerously, he felt rebuked for being young, inquisitive, and caring.

They were about an hour from home. Mahesh leaned forward and turned up the music. He had never been religious, but the devotional nature of the songs made him feel comfortable. He couldn't understand the words, but he could follow their movement, having heard them so often. They drove for a while without saying anything.

After about twenty minutes of silence, his father asked, "What are you going to do now?"

"I'm not sure. I thought I'd work at the store for a little while until I figured out what to do next." Working in the liquor store was the one thing he knew how to do well. And he wanted to know how his father would respond to him working there again.

From an early age, Mahesh and Nikhil had come straight from school to the store, where there was a little room in the back to play and do homework. Nikhil usually sat in the room by himself, while Mahesh sat near his mother behind the counter, where he could do his homework and watch her interact with customers. As soon as Nikhil was old enough, he started going straight home. Mahesh stayed. He liked spending time at the store. He felt useful and ahead of things, a feeling he didn't have during the school day.

By the time Mahesh was in the ninth grade, he rang up customers. And a few years later, he took over the ordering duties. He didn't have to look for a summer job; he already had one. College wasn't in the future. He had trouble paying attention in class, and he thought he already had a career: he was to be a small business owner. He graduated from high school and started full-time at the store. Things were fine for a while, but then he started arguing with his father. He did all the work, including the accounting, but his father still controlled the money and paid him a salary. Mahesh thought the salary was too small, even after his father increased it by a hundred dollars a week.

Mahesh had a couple of friends, neighborhood kids, who started bad and remained bad. They lived close by and went to high school with him. They came up with a plan. They knew of a vodka distributor who sold black-market liquor at a cheap price. They'd deliver it to Mahesh, and he'd sell it at full price. Near pure profit. Mahesh said no. They came back two weeks later. He knew it was a crime, but it seemed like low-impact crime. He wasn't killing anybody. He didn't do it to get back at his father. He did it because he thought he'd never get caught. He said he'd stop after the first batch. It was stupid, youthful logic. It went on for a full year. Together, the three made hundreds and thousands of dollars in profit. Mahesh began buying toys—clothes his parents could never afford, a new home stereo. And then the distributor was caught. He pointed his finger at the two friends, and they pointed the finger at Mahesh. The three made a deal and received jail time for grand theft. Mahesh's parents encouraged him to take the deal so that the sooner he began his sentence, the sooner they could put all this behind them.

"The restaurant might be better," the father said. "We need help there."

"That sounds great," Mahesh said. "It'll be perfect until I get back on my feet." Placing a time limit was an attempt to grasp some power, which he didn't have. Mahesh didn't blame his father for not trusting him in the store. At least he was being honest. Though Mahesh had looked forward to seeing his family, he was very nervous. He was ashamed of what he'd done. He didn't think his parents would push him away when he got out, but he wasn't quite sure how they'd react. When his father suggested the restaurant, he felt relieved that he was at least being integrated back into the family. Once he'd seen a movie where the owner of a restaurant spent the evenings eating, seating guests, and joking around with his friends. Maybe he could have this life at the restaurant.

Forty-five minutes later, they got off the freeway and waited for the stoplight at the end of the ramp. Ahead of them was their gas station, with cars coming and going. They turned left at the light and drove toward their house. To the right was a small shopping center with the restaurant. As they drove through the neighborhoods, Mahesh noticed the little things that disturbed the old familiarity: a house painted powder blue, a four-way stop where there used to be a two-way. This was the first time he was coming home after a prolonged absence. It was his version of a junior year abroad.

There were two cars parked in the driveway: his mother's Toyota and a white Honda Prelude. Both brothers felt the same nervous anticipation when they saw the Honda.

Shalini and Mahesh went to high school together, dated secretly for two years, openly for another, and split up at Christmas break during Shalini's first year at Berkeley. He visited her in the dorms but never felt comfortable in her new life and among her new friends. His parents were never keen on what they thought was the vague institution of *dating* but felt that Shalini was a perfect compromise.

They'd assumed the two would eventually get married. And when they didn't, his mother was very disappointed. She had liked Shalini and thought she could help Mahesh think beyond the liquor store and the daily grind of running a business. She'd noticed from an early age that he stayed within his comfort zone. She'd invited Shalini so that maybe this time her presence would prevent him from returning to that comfort.

When Nikhil arrived for his freshman year at Berkeley, he hadn't seen Shalini for some time. That first week of classes, he was walking across Sproul Plaza at noon. All around the perimeter, different student groups had set up tables, and the center was filled with students walking through, eating lunch, and talking. The sun was bright, and Nikhil was more overwhelmed than excited. He walked by the Indian Student Association table and recognized Shalini handing out flyers for the first meeting of the year. She was one familiar face out of five hundred. He'd always thought she was pretty, but now, away from the neighborhood, with her sunglasses propped a few inches above her forehead, she looked beautiful and glamorous, a symbol of the new life he wanted. They talked for a few minutes. Nikhil went to that first meeting, where she introduced him to her friends. He started going out with the group for Indian food on Shattuck Avenue and to parties off campus. Eventually, he developed an enormous crush on her, which he kept to himself. She was older and would never be interested, and she was his brother's ex-girlfriend. And of course these taboos intensified his interest. She was slightly pigeon-toed when she walked; he found himself walking with his right foot turned slightly inward. She drove without her shoes on; he did the same.

Nikhil and his father entered the house first, followed by Mahesh. The furniture in the living room—the floral couches, the cherry-wood center table, the daybed—was the same. The only new thing was a banner—a foot tall and ten feet wide—taped to the far wall: "Welcome Back, Mahesh." It was printed from the old dot-matrix printer in the office upstairs. Mahesh tried to figure out who'd put the banner up. Maybe his mother asked Nikhil to print it. She was always busy and often didn't think through her actions and decisions. By treating this like he had just returned from a hospital stay or a long period of travel, the father could avoid admitting that this was an unusual return. Maybe Nikhil did it on his own. His humor was biting at times. Whoever put it up, it did serve a purpose: the absurdity of it put Mahesh at some ease about being home. The banner got to the core of the problem. The parents could reluctantly deal with their children dating, drinking, and even doing drugs. But they didn't know how to handle prison. It made them feel like they were no different from other struggling immigrant groups.

His mother and Shalini stood below the sign.

"Hey, Ma," Mahesh said.

They'd never been a hugging family. But he went over and gave her an awkward hug. He'd missed his mother the most. It took all his strength to stop himself from crying. He went into the kitchen with her when she went back to lunch preparations, and he had a drink of water. Nikhil was talking to Shalini. Mahesh had acknowledged her, but she'd moved away so that he and his mother could talk.

He had not seen Shalini for well over two years, and they hadn't communicated while he was in jail. She was dressed in jeans and a well-pressed, white long-sleeve shirt. She looked like she'd been elsewhere in the years they were apart. He wanted to hug her, to feel her breasts on his chest, to place his nose in her hair and on her neck. But his father was standing there, and so instead he gave her a brief, quiet hug; their bodies barely touched.

Nikhil watched this and then went upstairs. The father followed him up.

This left Shalini and Mahesh alone in the living room. Mahesh had his suspicions that this privacy had been preorchestrated by his mother. They sat down on the couch, separated by a cushion but facing each other. Both were unsure of how much of their old intimacies they could assume. There was a period, before he went to jail and after they separated, when they had found a new way to interact. But now that measured familiarity seemed out of place.

"Did you graduate?" he finally asked.

"Yeah," she said. "Just a month ago."

"That's great. Are you still in that same apartment?"

"No. I've been living with my parents since graduation. I'm here for another month, and then I'll move into a place in San Francisco." Her parents lived about half a mile away. She said she was starting a job doing market research for a firm whose name Mahesh didn't recognize. They had broken up because every day she was getting further and further away from the world Mahesh understood. But right then, some of that old energy between them returned.

"How are you doing?" she asked.

"Good," he said. "But things are a little strange. I did just get out of jail." He said it to hear himself say it. "I don't know how to talk to them."

He wanted to keep talking to her, but his mother called them all in for lunch. "We'll talk after," he said as they went into the dining room.

The dining table was set with stainless steel dishes and bowls, and there were large glass serving bowls with steaming food all over the table. His mother had always been immaculate and thorough when they had people over for meals. He was happy to know that this skill was making her money. There was a moment of confusion about where people were to be seated before the father stepped in and pointed to seats. The father sat at one head, and the mother sat to the right of him. Mahesh sat to his father's left, and Shalini sat next to him. Nikhil and Shalini sat across from each other.

They'd never been much of a talkative family around the dinner table, but Mahesh thought it was his responsibility to keep things a little lively so that Shalini wouldn't feel uncomfortable.

"The food looks great," he said as he served Shalini. "How's the restaurant?"

His father answered before his mother could. He said it was doing very well, but he had nothing to do with it. Its success could be blamed entirely on the mother. His mother didn't quite get his use of the word *blame,* and after he said this, she kept her eyes on the table.

"Who's at the restaurant now?"

"I've hired a couple that are in charge of going to the wholesale market and buying things for the kitchen," his mother said. "They help with the cooking, and they're there now. I did the preparation for lunch this morning, and I'll go in a couple of hours for dinner. Sunday dinner is not so bad."

As the mother explained the day-to-day running of the restaurant, the prospect of working there sounded pretty good.

Nikhil started talking to Shalini. Mahesh wanted to concentrate on what his mother was saying, but he kept getting distracted by the conversation next to him. All he heard were names he didn't know. Nikhil had said nothing about this new life that included her. In their conversation, Mahesh's time away took concrete form: careers were taking shape, new friendships made and developed. All these years, Nikhil had expressed disdain for Mahesh's lack of ambition. But the one thing Mahesh had that Nikhil didn't was Shalini. She'd always been heading to new places but continued to like Mahesh despite it. Nikhil had had trouble with women. In high school, he never acted on anything because he always thought there was something better around the corner.

When they exhausted the conversation about the restaurant, Mahesh turned to his food and ate, as did his mother and the father. Shalini and Nikhil, however, continued to talk. Now he could concentrate on them. But nothing was instantly illuminated. People were taking jobs with companies Mahesh had never heard of and doing things in those companies that sounded foreign. Because Nikhil saw Mahesh listening, he exaggerated his happiness when he heard a new piece of news and insisted on communicating back in patois: "The CS folks were heavily recruited this year. HP, Intuit, Sun, Yahoo. Sanjay got three offers."

Mahesh couldn't tell if Shalini was interested or was being courteous.

Finally, he interrupted them. "What can I get you?" he asked Shalini.

She looked at her plate. She had barely touched anything. "Let me eat this first." For the next several minutes, they all ate quietly. And they would have gone on eating quietly were it not for Shalini's presence. Though she knew about the family dynamics, both Mahesh and Nikhil were self-conscious that she'd think that they were ultimately a quiet, boring family that had nothing to say to one another.

"Are you going to tell us a little about what you did in there?" Nikhil asked. There were plenty of things to talk about—Shalini's new job, Nikhil's school. But this was the question on all their minds.

"There's not much to tell. It was a minimum-security prison, so there wasn't the same kind of confinement you see on TV. I spent a lot of my time working in the library. And I played tennis. They had a prison league." None of this was new to any of them, except for Shalini. He'd talked about it when they came to visit, and he'd told Nikhil about it in his letters. "My backhand has gotten really strong."

"So how do you feel now?" Nikhil persisted.

"No different. Well, a little different. But I'm still the same person." Mahesh had a lot more to say, but he didn't want to talk about it in front of an audience. And the admiration he'd allowed himself to have of Nikhil was quickly evaporating. He was as smug as ever.

"You're still the same person that steals liquor. That's comforting." Nikhil hadn't intended to be so sharp, but it just came out. And once it did, he realized how much more he had to say. He and his parents had tiptoed around Mahesh since he'd been caught. They assumed that Mahesh recognized the gravity of his mistake and that he'd sufficiently dole out to himself the appropriate punishment, in jail time and in heavy doses of guilt. Their anger would only make his jail time more difficult. Now with prison behind them, Nikhil could say what they'd bottled up for two years. He had ruined his own life, but he'd ruined his family's as well. In one quick moment, the family's standing among their extended family and friends had dropped several notches.

"The least you could have done," Nikhil continued, "is worked on being a different person. We know you were reading and playing board games, but there was quite a bit we all had to do because of your mistakes. Mom had to postpone opening the restaurant for three months. It took us a while to get to where we're now. We were no pillar in the community, but we had a solid place in it. We all earned it together. Do you know they don't see many of their friends anymore? They stopped returning Mom's phone calls. They don't come to the restaurant. We opened it for everybody, but Mom had this idea that her friends would come by and she'd cook for them. You took all that away." He paused for a second and then continued. "Do you know how embarrassing it's been for me? My old friends just don't understand it. They think we're some kind of weird criminal family. And my new friends don't even know I have a brother. What should I say to them? 'Oh, by the way, here's the brother I haven't mentioned for the past two years.'" Nikhil was close to tears.

Mahesh looked around the table. He'd been waiting for his parents to stop Nikhil, but they just sat there. He didn't turn to face Shalini; but he could feel her discomfort, and he was not sure where she stood on all this. Did her friends in college know about him? What had she told the friends he'd met?

"What's this about us all earning it together?" Mahesh asked. "You spent no time in the store."

"I've spent plenty of time there the past couple of years."

"You're just making up for all the years you weren't there."

"Nobody asked you to spend so much time there," Nikhil said.

"Nobody asked me? Work needed to be done. I don't think you get it. You don't wait to be asked. We were supposed to work in the store. There was no money to hire somebody."

Mahesh turned to his parents because he wanted them to say something. Though the mother had wanted Mahesh to do something more ambitious, she'd never actively discouraged him from working in the store when they needed the help. The parents stayed silent. Neither took responsibility for the fact that they'd allowed him to work in the store all these years. They'd made good money from his labors.

"Don't blame me for wanting to do something different."

"I don't," Mahesh said, but he did. He was jealous of Nikhil's ease in school, and he was jealous of how much his parents allowed him to do what he wanted. They hadn't placed the same expectation on him to work in the store that Mahesh had felt.

There was a pause in the conversation.

"And what now?" Nikhil asked. "You barely graduated from high school. Maybe you should think about junior college. You can spend a couple of years there and figure out what you're going to do next. I know Dad said that you can work in the restaurant, but how long can that last before—"

Mahesh looked at Nikhil but didn't say anything.

"OK, that's enough," the father said.

They ate quickly and remained silent.

At the end of the meal, they all got up. And at the same moment, both brothers moved toward Shalini's plate, offering to take it in for her. The parents didn't think much of it and went into the kitchen. Though the two brothers and Shalini would never talk to one another about it, it was clear to all three that this was more than just a moment of good manners. And before either brother could offer to take her plate again, Shalini grabbed it and walked into the kitchen herself.

They all helped the mother clear the table and place the dishes in the dishwasher. When the activity subsided in the kitchen, no one was sure what to do next. They were all too tired to sit in the family room and talk. It was Shalini who broke up the party. "I should be getting home," she said. The mother made a feeble attempt at insisting she stay. The father said good-bye to her and went to watch TV in the family room. She gave the mother a quick hug and waved to Nikhil from across the room.

Mahesh and Shalini walked out the front door and went and stood against the trunk of her car, facing away from the house.

"Sorry about all that."

"I probably shouldn't have come," she said.

"No, no. I was happy when I saw your car outside." He wasn't sure how truthful an answer he'd get, but then he asked anyway. "Were you embarrassed of me too?"

"No," she said. "Well, maybe a little at the beginning. I was just confused, and I didn't know how to react. Jail is so far outside my realm of experience. Your family probably felt the same. I still don't understand all of it."

Mahesh wondered if she was defending Nikhil. "I still don't, either," he said. "I tried to figure it out, but I think I just made a stupid mistake. The money felt good."

"I wish you and I had just talked about it. I could have visited."

"I'm glad you didn't. I didn't want to talk to anybody. I didn't really like the visits from Nikhil and my dad."

"Are you OK from all that?" she asked, pointing to the house.

"Not really. But I guess it was good for him to get it out."

"He's still a kid," she said. "He has all sorts of emotions running around, and I don't think he knows how to handle them yet."

He finally felt at ease about where she stood. There was much more he wanted to say to her, but he couldn't think of anything else right then. He was happy to be there with her.

"Have you been to my mom's restaurant?"

"No. My parents told me about it, but we felt awkward about going."

"I haven't seen it yet, but you should come by with your parents. I'm going to work there for a bit."

"That'd be great," she said and paused. "I don't want to meddle, but are you sure you want to work for your parents again?"

"I need to think about it. I'm not so happy with them right now, but it feels like the right thing to spend some time with them. I'm good at working in a small business, and I need to do something I'm good at right now."

"OK," she said.

"Can we also hang out a little? Maybe a movie."

"Sure. I'm on vacation for the next month."

This time, their hug was longer and more substantive.

She got in her car, backed out of the driveway, and left. Mahesh stood and watched the back of the car as it got further and further away. And when he turned around to go back in, he noticed Nikhil in his old bedroom window upstairs. He didn't know how long he'd been up there watching. He waved, and Nikhil waved back.

They stayed in their own rooms for the rest of the afternoon, while the parents went to the restaurant. Before the father left, he told Mahesh to come by the restaurant in the evening so that he could show him around. Nikhil left the house at five without saying a word, and Mahesh followed an hour later. He walked to the store first. Before, it was called Jay Vee Liquors, and now the sign simply read "Wine and Spirits." His uncle, his father's younger brother, was working there. He greeted Mahesh warmly, and they talked about the changes in the store.

"This place looks incredible," Mahesh said. The tiles had been replaced with a wood floor, and there was a large selection of wines. They no longer sold cigarettes, candy, or chips.

"Nikhil pushed for these changes. The wine was his idea."

"How's it selling?"

"The liquor is still the best business, but the wine is doing very good."

It had never occurred to him to make improvements because the old store brought in good income. He walked around the store for a few minutes and then walked out and headed toward the restaurant.

When he walked in, his father was warm and welcoming, more than he'd been all day. He introduced Mahesh to the two waiters and then took him back to the kitchen to introduce him to the two others who helped his mother. Mahesh had spent his whole life between the gas station and the liquor store and knew the feeling of being in a place owned by his parents. But the restaurant felt different. Now there were people from outside the family working for his family. He was the boss's son.

The brothers didn't make eye contact.

55

By 6:30, half the tables were full. There were twelve tables in all; it was a small restaurant. The father stood behind the bar in the back of the restaurant, serving up soft drinks and beer and settling the dinner bills. Mahesh stood close to his father, uncertain about what exactly he should do. When Mahesh asked, his father told him to relax and get a feel for things. Nikhil welcomed and seated the guests. He joked with them and seemed very comfortable as he handed them menus and took orders. Mahesh had never seen Nikhil interacting with customers. It was like watching him act in a play.

At one point, a couple came in, and there was a connection between them and Nikhil that was different from his interactions with other customers. He gave them one of the nicer tables by the window and then called Mahesh over.

"These are some of our best customers," Nikhil said to Mahesh. "This is the third time they've driven in from San Francisco." Mahesh smiled at them when Nikhil introduced him as his older brother.

"A real family restaurant, ey?" the man said.

Nikhil smiled and said yes. The two brothers then went to the back while the couple looked through the menu. And slowly, Nikhil stayed back and allowed Mahesh to seat the customers, take their orders, and bring out the food. Because of the novelty, Mahesh had a great time doing it. He liked the high energy the restaurant required. By 7:30, all of the tables were full. The father said that on Friday and Saturday nights, there were usually several parties waiting to be seated. "This is not that bad," he said.

The brothers didn't talk directly. But through the customers, they were beginning to start conversation again. Mahesh watched his brother as he ran around, welcomed customers, took orders, brought out food, and kept everyone happy. One of the waiters was not feeling well, and so Nikhil told him he could go home. Nikhil smiled a lot and ran and got whatever it was the customers asked of him. At one point, he was summoned over to a table where a man had eaten halfway through his meal.

"How's everything?" he asked.

"There's something wrong with the spinach. It doesn't taste right." Nikhil took the food back and, ten minutes later, brought out a newly prepared dish, along with a complimentary bottle of beer. Nikhil's smile didn't leave his face all night.

At the end of the night, the couple at the table near the window were the only ones left. Finally, when they got up, Nikhil went over to say good-bye and locked the door behind them. He accorded them a great deal of deference. He'd always been a little rebellious, even as he got good grades and maintained good relationships with everyone around him. He voiced his opinion when he thought it was necessary. He didn't follow rules and authority blindly. But now he was doing everything except bowing to the couple.

In Nikhil's mind, there was a fair exchange in all this. For all the food and the good service, these customers were paying for the apartment Nikhil rented in Berkeley and the Cadillac parked out front. Since Mahesh went to jail, Nikhil had been helping out a lot more. He had a very good business sense. The store next to the restaurant had just shut down, and he was talking to the landlord about renting it and collapsing the wall between them. Nikhil had gone through different phases, but he knew that he wanted to make money and lots of it.

With all the customers gone, the father turned up the background music. It was the same CD he'd played in the car. His mother was cleaning up in the kitchen, and Mahesh was clearing out the tables, replacing the tablecloths, and laying out new glasses and silverware. He sat down at each table because his feet were tired from all the standing. He was happy to feel the fatigue of a long night of work. At one point, he looked to the back of the restaurant, where his father and Nikhil were standing behind the bar, separating the cash from the credit card receipts. For years, he'd done the same at the liquor store, first with his mother and father and then by himself. The accounting of the day's earnings was the purest part of the day. The sight of his father and brother sharing that moment jarred his heart. He not only saw himself replaced but realized that Nikhil had exceeded the best part of himself.

He'd tried not to make too much of the changes that Nikhil had made, but now it was hard to ignore. He could manage the un-equal expectations his parents had placed on the two of them, but he couldn't manage this.

He quickly cleared off and reset the remaining tables.

. "How's it going?" his father asked from the back.

"With what?"

"The silverware."

"Fine," Mahesh said. "I'm done here."

And he was done. Now, not a month or two from now, but now.

Patrick Ewing's Father

I had recently moved to New York City for a new job. I was thrilled to be there, and I stared to take in the newness of it all. I liked to stare. I liked looking at how people dressed, the shoes they wore, the books they read, and the looks on their faces. I liked listening to the words and content of conversations, and I was particularly intrigued by disagreements and fights. And I liked to visualize the size and the look of women's breasts. It was easier in summer than in winter, but in the winter I could work with my imagination. Staring is like television—if you look around enough, you are bound to find something you like.

Initially, I couldn't get enough of the Hasidic Jews. And then it was the Puerto Ricans. There were even working-class Indians and Pakistanis. But I was told that nothing good could come from my staring habit. New Yorkers didn't like starers, particularly on the subway. A friend told me that men interpret a starer as a threat to their masculinity and as an invitation to *throw down*. Women, he added, equally interpret a starer as a threat to their masculinity and as an invitation to *throw down*.

I am a statistician, and I interpret large amounts of consumer data. I create patterns from the goods—cars, books, diapers—that consumers purchase. I worked for a company headquartered in San Francisco that was trying to expand its presence on the East Coast; I was one small part of the expansion. My boss asked me on a Monday morning if I wanted to move, and first thing Wednesday I told him I did. If I was destined to have such a decidedly unglamorous job, at least I could live in New York City. I moved because I wanted something new in my life.

I was on my way home from work one early evening, sitting on the subway, reading a John Grisham novel. In San Francisco, I drove everywhere and never took public transportation. Once I took the bus when my car was in the shop, and I saw three different people reading Grisham. Since then, I assumed Grisham was supposed to be read in the haze of one's commute. But the truth is that the book was a front, a place to set my eyes between glances.

We came to a stop, and I looked up to see who was coming on board. Two people entered my car. The first was a young woman who looked around and walked through the doors connecting the cars and went into the next section. I felt disappointed because I had just begun to appreciate eastern European women. The second was a black man who walked past and then came back and sat in one of the empty seats next to mine. The car was only half full because, as usual, I had gone into work early and left early. He looked very familiar when he passed the first time.

It was winter. He had on scuffed black work boots, faded black jeans, and a large beige canvas jacket. His layers made him seem soft above the waist. He was wearing a black cap, nylon on the outside to protect him from the rain and wooly on the inside to keep him warm, with two flaps that dropped past his ears. It was the type of cap that Elmer Fudd wore when he went hunting. The man had two plastic grocery bags filled with food—bread, eggs, a gallon of skim milk, various canned goods.

I consider myself a subtle starer, but twice I tried to take a look at his face, and twice he caught me.

He spoke first. "I'm his father," he said.

I looked up from my book, which I had stopped reading the second he walked in.

"What?" I said.

He turned and faced me directly. "Patrick Ewing is my son. *He looks just like me.*"

Now I could stare unabashedly.

"It's amazing," I said. Why was the father of a famous, wealthy basketball player riding around in the subway, buying his own groceries, wearing old workmen's boots?

"Patrick and I, we don't get along," the man said. He'd had this conversation before and knew what I was thinking before I could ask the questions.

"That's too bad," I said, which didn't begin to express it. His circumstance wasn't bad; it was catastrophic. Ewing had come from a humble family in the Caribbean, and now he was rich. But his father's life hadn't changed. He was still buying his own groceries and taking the subway home. And, worse, he was estranged from his son.

"Why?" I asked.

"You a reporter?"

"Oh, no. I'm just curious. I liked watching him play."

He shook his head, as if to brush off my last comment.

"There's nothing to tell," he said. "We don't get along. He's got his life, and I've got mine. We just don't agree on some things."

I wanted him to keep talking because he hadn't said exactly why they didn't get along. But I was a little afraid to push. There was something unstable in his manner—his eyes were not very steady. So I read my book, and he stared straight ahead. Several stops later, I got off the train.

As I walked from the subway stop to my apartment, I decided that I would check online when I got home. There had to be stories about Ewing and his father. They looked identical. He was Ewing as an older man. He had the same nose and that same mouthy smile with all thirty-two teeth intact. He was not nearly as tall as his son, but he had large hands with long, bony fingers. I was suspicious about his claims, but the more I thought about how he looked, the more probable the story seemed. Their resemblance was convincing. The father wasn't himself a celebrity, but he was close enough; and for a starer like me, a celebrity sighting was a divine moment.

When I got to my apartment, the phone was ringing.

"You're home." It was Mala calling from San Francisco. She sounded tentative.

"I just walked in." I was excited and wanted to tell somebody about my encounter, but Mala had probably never heard of Patrick Ewing. I didn't have the patience to explain who he was, nor did I have the patience, just then, for her. She neither knew nor cared about celebrities. And though she had not said it, she had a slight disdain for my interest in them.

"How's everything?" she asked.

We'd spoken only a handful of times since I arrived, and it was getting more and more difficult to get past the small talk.

"Fine," I said.

"What have you been up to?"

"Work has been busy. And there's quite a bit to do here at night." The second I said it, I wanted to take it back. But I didn't. I was surprised that I felt fine with that small bit of cruelty.

Most things in my life could be handled with greater care and more thought. I lived in the Bay Area for many years and loved it until my last year there. To visitors, I boasted about the proximity of the mountains and the ocean, but I had no desire to visit what I myself thought was thin mountain air and cold water. I read a story about the elderly in Chicago dying in their apartments because they couldn't afford air-conditioning. I learned that the average summer temperature in a part of South India hovered around 115 degrees. I was sick of how the weather made everyone in San Francisco so self-satisfied.

But I assumed I'd never leave the Bay Area. Leaving seemed counterintuitive. Sure, the heat would be interesting for a while, but the novelty couldn't last. And I had most of my friends and family in the area. Several months before that Monday when my boss offered me the transfer, he asked if I'd be willing to relocate to New York. I smiled and said I'd consider it. At first, I didn't. But then I let myself think about it. I knew the Bay Area so well, but it was the only place I knew as an adult. How had I become so provincial?

As it turned out, my boss's timing that Monday morning was impeccable. Mala and I had been seeing each other for about six months, but for the last few weeks we'd been fighting. She was not so angry that it had happened; she was angry that it had happened twice. I didn't know what else to say but sorry. Mine is not a lawless heart. I went alone to a friend's party because Mala was out of town. I was drinking a beer and staring at a stunningly beautiful woman. She stared back. I was startled that I was the object of instant desire. We spent that night together, and I went back the second time to make sure that she hadn't made a mistake.

Mala and I had a long conversation on the Monday night after my boss made the actual transfer offer. I kept repeating that it was good for my career. But really I was ready for a break. The question of her moving with me hovered over our entire conversation. But all night, we talked around the topic and spoke only vaguely about our future together. We agreed that the distance would help us figure out how to proceed.

We'd had a good thing, and since I had moved to New York, that vagueness about our future had been of great service. Whenever I felt lonely and thought the move was a mistake, the possibility of going back to Mala gave me the boost to ride through the difficult hours. I could always return to California and resume the life we had. She was a beautiful safety net.

"I know it's last minute," she said, "but I'm going to be in New York later this week. I have meetings on Thursday and Friday, and I'm not flying back until Sunday morning. My Saturday is free. I'd like to see you."

I wanted more time to devise an answer, though it was clear to me that I was doing fine without her. She'd interpret the two of us meeting as a sign of our relationship moving forward. She did not like the ambiguity nearly as much as I did. Then the image of the man I'd just met on the train flashed through my mind. I wanted to tell Mala that I was in a new place and seeing new people.

"Sure," I said. "That'd be great." As much as I was ready to move on, I had to see her when she was flying all the way across the country. I was in no mood to have the big conversation, but it needed to happen. I suggested we meet for lunch to defuse the expectations of a Saturday-night dinner. And the question of her staying with me never came up. I assumed her firm was paying for a hotel through the weekend.

After getting off the phone, I forgot to check for Ewing stories online.

A few days later, I was on the subway coming home from work, and Ewing's father got on again. Did this happen often? Did people repeatedly meet randomly on the subway? After we made eye contact, he came and sat down near me. He was wearing the same clothes as the previous day.

"Hello again," I said. "Do you take this train often?" It sounded like a pickup line.

"There's a little shopping area where I go sometimes to pass the time."

"My name is Sunil," I said, offering my hand.

"Sumil?"

"No, Su-nil."

"Hello, Neil, I'm Carl." I didn't like my name shortened, but I didn't say anything. Finding a way to ease the strangeness of the strange struck me as being very American.

He told me about the different shops that he visited—a vegetable market, a music store, an electronics shop. He said he could spend hours looking at TVs and stereos. This was of little interest to me, and after he had talked about shopping for several minutes, I tried to steer him away from the topic. "I was interested in what you were saying a couple of days ago."

"I'm sure you are," he said.

This comment struck me as a little sharp.

He looked around the car. It was half full, but there was no one sitting close to us. He looked around a second time and then began: "My wife, Dorothy, and I worked very hard in Jamaica. Kingston was nice, but there was not enough there, and we wanted to do something for our kids. Five girls and two boys—Carl Jr. and Patrick and the girls. We moved to Cambridge in Massachusetts, and we both worked. I worked as a mechanic, and Dorothy took whatever job she could find. We brought the kids one by one. Patrick didn't come until four years after we first arrived. There was just not enough money to bring him." He didn't have a Jamaican accent, but there was a hint of something. And his story sounded polished, as if he had already told it to Barbara Walters. It was the stuff of the great American journey, but I knew that the journey had ended badly for Carl.

He continued. "Dorothy worked hard and then one night had a big heart attack. *Massive.*"

I had never lost somebody so close to me, and I couldn't imagine what he felt when he remembered his wife. I could only notice his looking away, the drop in his voice when he said "massive." He must have missed her. And now he had lost his son.

"Then it was just me and the kids. Patrick had started playing basketball. Picked it up for the first time when he was twelve and ran with it. Those years in high school and college were tough. Do you remember all the taunting when he played? They said he couldn't read. Bastards. They were animals." Here was an emotion I recognized. There was fury in his eyes, the way there was fury in my mother's eyes when she used her choice and only profanity: "Bastards." It always scared me when she said it.

"Sure," I said. I didn't really remember him in his early years, as a high school standout and at Georgetown, though I had heard that he had trouble then. Spectators threw banana peels on the court and called him a monkey. But there were those glorious years in New York: the big man running up and down the court, his large hands palming the ball, the sweat pouring down his face as if he had just come in out of the rain.

As Carl spoke, the story about the move of the big family from Jamaica seemed familiar. There had been the Ewing myth about the hardship and the turn away from it in basketball. I couldn't figure out whether I already knew some of these details or was just hearing them for the first time through Carl's mouth. There were so many of these immigrant stories on TV and in the newspapers.

"You know the rest," he continued. "First at Georgetown and then the years in the Garden. I loved the Garden. I never got tired of going in there. I liked to get there early. Spike Lee would come by, and we'd talk about the new movie he was making."

I wanted to hear more about Spike Lee and the other stars he would see there. Had he seen Woody Allen? "And so when did things go sour?"

"It was when he wanted to be the man," he said. "He had the money, and he was buying houses and cars. He was buying us houses and cars. I wanted a Cadillac, and he got me a Cadillac. The cars were fine, and we all deserved it. But I am the man. I worked to get us here, and I worked so that he could play basketball. And now he wants to walk around like he's the one in charge. I dealt with it for years because I thought it was a phase that he would grow out of. But I had enough when it didn't stop. I didn't work this hard to have my kid walk around and pretend like he did all this. *I did all this.*" He was not angry. His voice stayed level throughout the conversation. Perhaps he had told this story to enough people that it didn't make him angry anymore.

"That's too bad," I said.

"What's too bad?"

"That the two of you don't get along." The second I said this, I knew I had said the wrong thing. "Well, I mean, it's too bad that he hasn't given you the proper respect." I could see Carl approved of this response.

"But does it make you sad?" It seemed so girly to ask how it made him feel, but I really wanted to know.

"Sadness is not the point," he said. "I want us to get along. What father doesn't want that, after all that we have been through? And I like the luxury I feel around him. But all that is material, or immaterial. I came from nothing, so going back to nothing doesn't seem that bad." He sounded like a Buddhist. "But all that I have is what I think is right and wrong. If I give that up, I have nothing left. Patrick is wrong. He needs to recognize that I am still his father." He paused for a second and then said, "Here's my stop."

Carl's stop was the one after mine. I told him that I had missed my station, and we both got out of the train and walked up the stairs. I could easily have walked to my place from his stop, but standing there, away from the subway train, I didn't want to follow Carl into the street.

"I'm going to wait for the train on the other side. It's too far for me to walk."

We said good-bye, and he headed toward the exit. I looked around but didn't immediately see where I needed to go to catch the train back. Carl noticed me looking around and took a step back toward me. "Here, I'll show you," he said. I let him show me. I was comfortable in the subway stations I regularly used, but new stations brought back the fear and disorientation I had felt when I first arrived in the city. Perhaps Carl had sensed this.

We walked about forty feet and stood at the top of the stairs that led to the correct platform. I wasn't sure whether he wanted to talk further.

"You seem like you're new to the city."

"Well, I've just never been to this station."

"But how long have you been living here?"

I had a rule to never let on that I was new, but it seemed silly to maintain a front with Carl, who had told me so much about his life.

"A couple of months," I said.

"I figured. You're a lot friendlier than the people I regularly meet on the subway. Where are you from? The Midwest? Iowa, I bet."

I couldn't tell if he was messing with me. Of all the ways I had described myself, and had been described by others, the Midwest had never entered the realm of possibility. What was it about the way I looked, and the things I said, that led Carl to the Midwest? "Further west," I said. "California."

"Ah, California." He said it twice and nodded his head as if this one piece of information explained everything about me. "Of course, I've been to Los Angeles a couple of times. Whew. That's a big, beautiful ocean. You from LA?"

"No. San Francisco."

"Now, why would you leave that good weather and all those beautiful women and come to New York?"

Before I could answer him, he had his own response.

"You came for the adventure, didn't you? Got a little sick of the same old thing. Looking for a new job. No, wait. You left a pretty wife behind to start a new thing."

I felt like I was talking to a fortune-teller. He had cast his net wide enough to hit on the larger issues of anyone's life. But there was something eerie about how he made all the right guesses. "There was somebody, but not a wife. You know, even California stops being beautiful if you stare at it too long."

Carl had a big smile on his face.

I was happy to hear the train coming. I said good-bye and went down to the platform. I wanted to be angry at Carl for the pleasure he took in predicting my situation. I had respectfully listened to him and hadn't laughed at the change in his fortunes. And I would have been angry were it not for the fact that he was right about almost everything. I couldn't be angry that he'd reduced me to a type. I had accomplished that all by myself.

As I thought about it, back on the train, Carl's story seemed so sad. It was a sadness I thought I understood. After all the success, the unimaginable success, how could they fight? Patrick, it seemed, had crossed that very thin line between being the successful son who had made his father proud beyond any measurable means and being the son who had outgrown his father. I couldn't blame Carl for feeling what he felt. No one deserved to be the one who was outgrown. His fatherhood, once so essential, had been reduced to a phase.

Yet how could I blame Patrick? Little about his story resonated with my own experiences. I got along well with my father, perhaps because I had not yet outgrown him. I came to the United States with my family when I was quite young, and now we had stability, but nothing like the riches the Ewings had. Patrick had worked very hard and had the right to live the life he wanted, the right to be the big man.

When I got home, I turned on my computer and dialed into the Internet. I didn't doubt Carl's story. There was nothing excessive in what he described. I just wanted to know more.

I typed "Patrick Ewing's Father" into a search engine, and it came up with a bunch of different stories. I began with one that seemed promising: "No Ring, but a strong circle of family and friends." I had not kept up with things. I didn't know that Ewing had recently retired. He played for the Knicks and then spent a year in Orlando, and then, after seventeen seasons in the NBA, he announced his retirement. There had been a tribute for him in New York recently, and everyone was there—old coaches, people he had played with, his family. The article discussed how through all the highs and lows of his career, his family had remained the bedrock for Patrick. He and his father, Carl, were very close. Had the family kept up a good front so as not to look bad in the press? Perhaps the fight was very recent. The story recounted the exact tale that Carl had told me earlier. They all moved from Jamaica, the kids coming one by one; they lived in a five-room house in Cambridge with nine people; Patrick played at the Cambridge Rindge and Latin School and then chose Georgetown over Boston College. The fans in Boston were brutal to him when he came to town with the Hoyas. They were angry that a Boston local had decided not to play for BC, and they were angry that he beat them handily on the court. His family was with him through it all.

It seemed strange that Carl wasn't dressed well and took the subway with his groceries. But of course he was too proud to take money from his son. The article talked about how private the family was and how they, particularly Carl, seldom granted interviews. He had, however, spoken to this reporter and said he lived happily now, still in Cambridge, on the top floor of a duplex. His other son, Carl Jr., lived below him.

I met Mala in the lobby of the Hilton near Rockefeller Center at noon. I was quite nervous to see her. On my way there, I thought about the different things I was going to say, most of which revolved around the reasons why we couldn't be together. It took the first sight of her—the short black hair, the high cheekbones—to remind me that she was an attractive woman. We hugged and then somehow ended up kissing for several long seconds. I had missed this type of warmth in the past few months. And then we backed away from each other. I had certainly not planned to kiss her. Mala seemed surprised as well.

"Nice hotel," I said, as I looked around the large lobby. She hated big hotels. The few times we'd traveled together, she insisted on staying in smaller places, even though they were more expensive.

"The office is close by," she said. "At least it's convenient."

"Shall we go?" It was a very sunny day, and the temperature was in the high forties. I hadn't lived in New York long enough to know that this was an ideal winter's day. "Are you hungry?"

"Not really," she said. "I slept in and had breakfast late."

"We could walk around for a while and then eat. Is there something in particular you want to see?"

"I've never been to the Met. That's close, isn't it?"

We took a cab there, and when we got out in front of the museum, there were people sitting all over the steps. It was warmer than it had been for a couple of weeks. Inside, the line for admission was long. We decided to take a walk through Central Park instead. It felt like a touristy thing to do, but I was still, after all, a tourist.

Like the museum, the park was packed with people, though there was more room to spread out. I had walked around this part of the park once before by myself, and I remember thinking that the walk would have been better had I not been alone. I hadn't pictured myself with Mala necessarily. Just not alone. Now with Mala, it felt more natural to walk among the couples, the young families, and the clusters of friends. As we walked, I didn't know exactly how to interact physically with her. We certainly weren't going to hold hands, but walking a few feet apart didn't feel right either. We ended up somewhere in the middle. It was Mala who moved slightly away when we seemed to be getting too close.

"Did you get your work done?"

"Yeah," she said. "But the real work will get done when I get back."

"Why'd you come on such short notice?" I heard the reproach as it came out of my mouth. "Not that I mind. I'm glad you're here."

"The partner I do a lot of work for needed some help on a case he's been working on out here and asked me to come along at the last minute."

We walked through the park for about half an hour. As we walked, we slowly gained some of the ease we used to have. I told her about work, about how I was going on sales calls and feeling more comfortable in that role. When we had discussed the possibility of my move, I told Mala I wanted to go to New York because I'd have some opportunity to work with the marketing group. I was still the technical guy on sales visits, but I was doing something new.

She caught me up on some mutual friends. I was going to tell her about my encounter with Carl, but I didn't. If there had been even a hint of indifference in her voice and manner, it would have blemished the joy I got from those interactions.

Then we headed toward Madison Avenue, another bit of New York that was far more interesting with a companion. We window-shopped and walked through Barney's and Bergdorf Goodman before we ended up at Brooks Brothers. I needed some new clothes, and the one time she and I had been shopping together, she helped me pick out some nice things. And as we chose shirts for me to try on, it felt like we were back in San Francisco. We went upstairs with the shirts and picked out several pairs of pants. When I came out of the dressing room in an orange shirt and a pair of black slacks, Mala walked up to me to see how they fit.

"The shirt looks great. How do the pants feel?" she asked.

"Pretty good. How do they look?"

She looked at them and then placed her hand on the pleats to show that the pants were a little baggy below the waist. My body stiffened a little, and she quickly removed her hand. "I'll check if they have some without pleats," she said and walked away. I bought two pairs of pants, with pleats but in a smaller size, and several shirts.

Our walk through the park and the shopping felt like a perfect little domestic outing. Both of us were hungry now, and we ended up at a sushi place. For the first time that day, there were no other stimuli to distract us. We sat down and ordered our meal.

"What do you do on the weekends?" she asked.

"I haven't had that many weekends here. For the first few, I put my place together. There are some people at work that I hang out

71

with. And there's this college buddy of mine who lives here. He has a bunch of his friends he's introduced me to." Even though there was nothing happening with the people I'd met, I tried to stay as vague as I could.

"Are you seeing anyone?"

For the past two hours, we'd stepped around the conversation we needed to have, and I was glad to get to it. "Of course not." I felt like I was on some moral perch as I said this.

She took a sip of her Coke and then continued. "I'm beginning to see someone."

I didn't immediately respond because I thought she'd elaborate, but instead she drank some more of her Coke. It was her turn to be vague. She had every right to be seeing someone else. I was the one who'd cheated on her and the one who had been unwilling to define our relationship. She didn't owe me anything. But that didn't stop my heart from thumping in my ears. In that instant, Mala became incredibly desirable.

"Oh," I finally said. "I'm glad."

"Are you?"

Just then the waiter came over with two bowls of steaming miso. I was grateful for the diversion. I took a few careful sips and then said, "Actually, I'm not."

"What do you want me to do?"

"I have no idea." I was honest. I couldn't figure out if she was telling me this as a way of ending our relationship or as an opportunity for me to step up and commit to her more substantially. I looked straight at her, but nothing in her face gave me an answer. But knowing what I knew of her, I was sure she wouldn't try to get me back by finding someone else. "What if I told you that I could get transferred back, or we tried to get you transferred here?"

"That's the problem, Sunil. You don't know what you want. Do you want to get transferred back? Do you want me to get transferred here? You've had two months to make some attempt at keeping this going. I'm the one who always ends up calling."

"Can we just drink this soup for a little bit?" I needed a few minutes. I had enjoyed New York a lot more in the past few hours than I had at any time in the past two months. It was an exciting place, with a lot of people, but I'd had some pretty lonely nights. There was no joy in going to bars with people you were just getting to know. I wasn't suddenly in love with Mala, but it was hard to let her go. "Can we see if you can get transferred here? I'd really like that."

"Maybe I misspoke. I'm not asking you to make a decision now about me moving or you coming back." She paused for a second. "You cheated, and then you up and left. I've had a couple of months to realize just how ridiculous you've been. It hasn't been easy, but I've felt calmer and more settled since you've been gone. I work a lot to keep my mind occupied."

"Do you work with him?" I sometimes had the feeling that I wasn't quite successful enough for Mala. I never liked the guys I met from her work.

"I don't want to talk about him."

Mala was willing to make herself vulnerable. It was the thing that I admired when I was first getting to know her. But once someone messed with those emotions, she backed away. Her relationships with both her mother and sister were distant. I was surprised it had taken her this long to distance herself from me. But now I could hear it in her voice.

"Why did you tell me about your fling?"

I thought about it for a few seconds. Mala could slice up everything I said, analyze the parts, and put it back together.

"Because I felt bad, and it was the right thing to do. I figured that if I told you, we could deal with it and then continue on."

"You felt bad, but not because you cheated on me. You felt bad because you wanted to break up, and this was the easy way to do it. You let me do the breaking up."

"That's not true." I hated it when Mala was arrogant about her command of my emotions, and I hated how she made me feel like a typical man.

The waiter brought us our food, but I was in no mood to eat.

We both picked at our plates for several long minutes. Mala didn't look angry, but she was far from the playfulness she'd had when she was pulling out different shirts for me to try on at Brooks Brothers.

"Are you hungry?" I asked.

"Not really."

I called over the waiter and requested the bill. He looked at the untouched food and then looked at us. "Is everything OK?"

"Yes," I said.

I offered to walk her back to her hotel, but she said she'd be fine. We hugged good-bye, and this time it was quick and simple. As I was heading back home, I kept telling myself that it hurt now, and it did hurt, but soon I'd be glad that Mala had said no. I could only start anew after I completely broke with the old. I kept telling myself that.

Early the following week, Carl got on my subway car again, and I realized that he, too, had a ritual for riding the subway. I always rode in the last car because I figured that when a head-on collision occurred—and I knew that it eventually would with all the different lines crisscrossing—I would be the least affected. I could walk out and see the damage in front of me. Carl must have had something similar in mind, because he always boarded my car.

He stepped in and looked around, and when we made eye contact, he came over and sat down.

"What's up, Neil?"

"Nothing," I said. "Just a long day of work."

He didn't ask me about my work, so I didn't say anything. We sat in silence as the subway picked up speed. So there we were, and we had to make some conversation until I reached my stop. There was this one thing nagging me.

"You mentioned last week that you all moved to Cambridge when you first came. Have you lived in New York since Patrick came to play here?"

"No," he said. "I still have a place in Cambridge, where I live most of the time. But sometimes I get a little bored of the routine, and so I come down and spend a few weeks here with one of my daughters. She lives here." He paused and then continued. "I talked to Patrick last night. He called."

I wanted to ask the things I wanted to know when we first met. What is he like? What kind of car does he drive? How big is his house? I wanted us to talk about the easy stuff, and I was relieved that I had resolved my one doubt.

"He said he wants to see me. Now that he's not playing, he has more time, and he wants to spend it with me."

"When are you going to see him?"

"I don't know if I am," he said. "I want him to think about what he's done. I'll see him, but not just yet. He needs to learn. He was such a good kid. I remember watching him in high school. He was still playing with kids even though he had become a man. He dominated them, and then we would talk after the games. I didn't know much about basketball, but there were things that I picked up. Just sitting there watching my boy play his heart out, it was the greatest joy for me."

I looked at him, and his eyes seemed to have watered. He was quiet for a moment, and then he asked, "Do you want to see some pictures?"

"Sure," I said.

He reached into his back pocket and got out an old leather wallet. It was packed with receipts and notes written on scraps of paper. He opened it, and inside was a set of card-sized plastic sheets, all held together by a binding. I used to have one in the first wallet I owned in elementary school. In it, I placed my library card; a slip of paper with my name, address, and phone number; and a photo of myself taken at picture day in the fourth grade. I didn't have anything else to put in.

Carl held his wallet between us and showed me his pictures. They were all cutouts of Patrick Ewing from the newspaper and from color magazines like *Sports Illustrated*. The first picture was one of Ewing from his Georgetown days, but the rest were from his days with the Knicks. He took each one out so that I could get a better look. The edges of the pictures were sloppy and uneven.

"Patrick gave me this one after his rookie season with the Knicks." As he handed me the picture, his hand touched mine, and he kept it there for a few seconds longer than necessary. I looked at him, and his eyes were still a little moist, though the look in them had changed.

Carl had been so convincing. And I had been so willing to be convinced. Somewhere in the back of my mind, I'd thought this would all lead to a brief, friendly meeting with Patrick. I wondered what Carl's apartment looked like. I imagined that it was small and filled with magazines and newspapers. Weren't all New York apartments cramped and full of things? Was there anyone there with him? There may have been family at some point, but they were all probably gone now, dead or moved away. And was his name even Carl?

At first I thought he was asking me to let him have the world he'd created. But I'd believed him before he brought out the pictures. He didn't need to show them to me. Apparently he wanted me to see his real life. And what he had was far less than I had, but there I was looking for people on the subway the same way he was.

"Those are really wonderful pictures, Carl," I said, handing them back.

He put them in his pocket. "Maybe I'll see him," he said. "It will be nice."

"Yes, it would be."

We rode in silence, and I didn't feel any need to fill it. When my station approached, I got up and shook his hand. We avoided each other's eyes, as if we'd said a little too much, a little too quickly. I got off the train and ran up the stairs, feeling sad—for Carl, for losing Mala, for the fool I had been, for everything. As I walked home, I thought about the choices I'd made and the ones I'd failed to make. I thought about what choices I could still make, and I saw it would be a while before I'd find a way to leave New York.

A Housewarming

Diligence afforded Rohit Mehta some luxuries—occasional rounds of golf, a twenty-two-hundred-square-foot house in a well-spaced suburban development, a treadmill and a TV in the garage. On the weekends, he spent time with his family, playing doubles, growing zucchinis and peaches in the backyard, and taking weekend trips to Tahoe and Carmel. His wife, Gayatri, whom he'd first met when he was three and then married at twenty-five the summer before his last year in business school, took care of all household issues. How could he not love a woman who made him one perfect sunny-side-up egg every morning, did his taxes in April, and had never expected him to change diapers when their children were young? He showed affection toward his son and daughter though felt a little unnatural in the act. During football season, he spent a good part of Sunday afternoons on his couch. That Rohit's parents had left Bombay for a new country so that their children might have a better life had, until recently, kept at bay any discomfort and dissatisfaction he may have had with the details of his success.

Then one late Sunday afternoon, Rohit, Gayatri, and the two kids were driving in their Lexus two miles up the hill from their house to Sanjay Rao's housewarming party. Rohit and Gayatri knew Sanjay and his wife, Kamala, through mutual friends, though not very well.

"Shit," Rohit said, louder than he intended, when he matched the address on the invitation with the number on the house.

The front side of a small hill had been sliced off to clear the room for a house that was several times larger than Rohit's. A mansion on a bulldozed hill. The front of the house had one large gable in the center and two smaller gables on either side. The façade was gray brick, impractical for both the East Bay's mild winters and hot summers. Though he'd never actually seen one in person, Rohit associated the style with English manor houses. There was a large fountain—a *Venus de Milo* with water spraying out of her arms—in the center of a circular driveway. And to the left of the house was a tennis court still under construction. Rohit knew insurance could be good business, but he didn't think it was this good.

"Their website must get more hits than ours," said their fourteen-year-old daughter, Neha, from the back, as if she'd read Rohit's mind.

Many of the guests had already arrived, and Rohit had to park on the next block. As Gayatri and the kids walked ahead, Rohit lagged behind. They waited for him at the front door to catch up.

"Go ahead," Rohit said, as he neared them.

His son, Arvind, rang the doorbell.

Sanjay's wife, Kamala, answered the door. She was wearing a dark, sapphire-blue sari embroidered along the edges in gold. The intricate workmanship was worth the compromised vision of at least one child, if not an entire orphanage. But even more remarkable were the large diamond studs, the size of small peanuts, in her ears. In those first few seconds at the door, Rohit took in the majesty of Kamala's sari and wanted to run it between his index finger and his thumb to feel the quality of the silk. Standing there, the image of his mother slipped into his mind. She had good, subtle taste and always took great pride in her saris. He could picture the closet in his mother's room, with the saris neatly folded and piled ten high.

Gayatri didn't wear saris much anymore, except on rare occasions. The one she was wearing now—beige with a small, intricate pattern on the borders sewn in a lighter-colored thread—was not nearly fancy enough to be noticed. Rohit wondered what was wrong with calling a little attention to oneself?

"Rohit, Gayatri, so nice to see you." Twenty years in America and Kamala still had a British-inflected accent that she cultivated to show that Mumbai–London–San Francisco was her natural triangle of travel.

The marbled entryway was the size of Rohit's living room. In the center sat a small round table crowded by a bouquet of purple orchids. The large living room was furnished formally with an ornate, cherry-wood center table, matching coffee tables, and white couches with cherry-wood trim. At one end of the room was a black Steinway. Covering the entire floor was a Persian rug, which alone must have cost twenty thousand dollars. And another orphanage.

"The kids can go downstairs if they like," Kamala suggested. "There's food there and other kids."

Neha and Arvind stood there. "Go ahead," Gayatri said. "We'll be up here."

Arvind remained close to his father. Rohit quickly ran his fingers through his son's hair and steered him toward Neha, who'd begun to head downstairs.

Sanjay walked into the entryway. He was wearing khakis, a maroon Nike golf shirt that hung on him well, and a pair of loafers. Rohit thought the shirt was handsome.

"Rohit, it's so nice to see you." They shook hands. "Please go ahead inside, and I'll be there in just a minute."

Sanjay's handshake was soft and his manner gentle. Though lean in the rest of his body, he had a bit of a belly. In this, he and Rohit shared the same struggle. Rohit couldn't figure out how such softness had gotten him this house.

Kamala led them to the back of the house where a cavernous area, with two crystal chandeliers hanging from high, beamed ceilings, encompassed the kitchen and family room. About fifty people were gathered in small clusters. They were mostly Indians. The women wore fancy saris and the men khakis and ironed button-down shirts. The men seemed at ease, as if owning such a house was a part of life's natural progression. Most of them were doctors and engineers: old-economy stiffs. Rohit scanned the room and resented how easily laughter escaped their mouths.

"Food and drinks are on the dining table and the kitchen counter," Kamala said. The doorbell rang. "I'll be right back," she said and disappeared.

"Why doesn't she just leave the door open?" Rohit asked Gayatri and then answered his own question. "It's an opportunity for the guests to admire her sari and diamonds."

"Why have you noticed her sari?" Gayatri asked.

Rohit thought about the question. Why haven't you?

The buffet service was set up like at an Indian restaurant. There were five different kinds of vegetables, lamb in a creamy spinach sauce, chicken vindaloo, and tandoori chicken, each in a silver-plated cauldron, set on an individual, slow-burning flame. Two women at the stove made fresh rotis and puris. The dishes looked like they had been made in small, fresh batches, the oil properly saturated through slow, deliberate cooking. Gayatri put some channa and a large, palm-sized puri on her plate.

To the side, there was a full liquor cabinet.

"I'm going to have a drink first," Rohit said.

Gayatri looked at him, and Rohit held her gaze. I need it today, he thought. He needed it because decisions had to be made, and a bit of alcohol might give him clarity.

A year earlier, Rohit and Gayatri had envisioned allthingsindian .com as a one-stop destination: "Shopping in India without the heat or the hassles." They set up suppliers and made a trip to India to buy stock. Though Gayatri thought they should hire someone with more experience, Rohit insisted on hiring his young cousin Jai to design the website. They didn't search for funding because they wanted to keep things small and manageable. They cleared out half of the garage for inventory and shipping material, and in one of the upstairs bedrooms, they set up an office. After the site went live, there was an initial burst of orders, mostly from friends and relatives. Then things quieted down. Rohit spent some time and money on advertising, which resulted in a short spike in business. Then things quieted down again. They didn't know whether to blame the poorly designed website or their overestimation of consumer interest in India. Indians, it seems, were more interested in shopping for spices and food in stores where they interacted with other Indians.

After six months, they had a small, steady stream of customers but weren't breaking even. Their savings was quickly running out. Gayatri thought that Rohit was on an extended leave of absence from his old job and could return whenever he wished. He hadn't told her that several months before, he'd been given an ultimatum. In response, he'd turned in his resignation, certain that the website would succeed.

Fresh from business school, Rohit had joined a telecommunications company, where he'd worked for a decade. He'd seen friends from his school days succeed in start-up after start-up. There was plenty of success for the taking. Why not him? It was a dream to start something yourself, to see it grow. Sure, selling for a couple of million would be great. But the act of starting a company had the long view in mind. Living the middle-management life hadn't been all that bad. A decent 401K, an inheritance for the children if you'd been judicious. But wasn't it worth the chance and the effort to look back and know that you'd created *something* and done it well? On seeing the new website's mock-up, he'd begun to feel the same entrepreneurial excitement that led him to an MBA. And feeling Rohit's excitement, Gayatri wanted to be involved too. In India, she'd earned a bachelor's degree in commerce, though the skills she'd acquired there did not easily translate to the American market.

That morning before they went to the housewarming party, they had made their customary Sunday-morning love.

"I can go either way," Gayatri said after, pulling the duvet up to her neck. "The numbers aren't so good. They've never really been good."

"Close it up?" he said. "Are you crazy? I think we can easily make one more push. We don't need to make any big decisions right now." He was annoyed that Gayatri was talking purely in terms of numbers. Even though they revealed a certain crystalline truth, there was more at stake than Gayatri realized. He was angry at her and at his insistence on sticking to one company and one industry for so long. Perhaps different types of experience would have given him the knowledge to make the business work.

"If you think that we need to make another push, I'm with you," Gayatri said. "All I want is for us to make an active decision. I don't want to keep doing something based on our inability to decide."

Make an active decision? He wondered if this is what she thought of him. She'd said this about him before, and it sounded like she was talking about someone else.

Rohit stood in front of Sanjay's liquor cabinet, stocked with some thirty bottles of every possible type of high-end liquor. The only open bottles were several brands of scotch, including a half-empty bottle of Johnnie Walker Blue. At $250 a bottle, he'd never tasted it, and there it was just sitting there, unguarded. There were several open boxes with brand-new scotch glasses. He took one and poured himself a good amount. It tasted smooth, but besides that, he did not have the vocabulary to describe what he was drinking.

He didn't recognize many people around the room. In one corner near the fireplace, he saw the Menons and the Sharmas, the two couples they often spent time with on the weekends. Gayatri was already there.

Both Ram Sharma and Anand Menon were sipping scotch. Ram was a cardiologist and Anand a structural engineer. They had consistent work lives, and the only volatility they allowed themselves was in their dealings with the stock market.

"What's Sanjay thinking?" Rohit asked, speaking quietly.

"He's trying to impress us, and I'm pretty impressed," Ram said. "Very oaky," he continued, exaggerating an Indian accent, holding up his glass.

Ram reached over and tapped Rohit on his side belly, assuming an intimacy that doctors could get away with. "We need to get that doubles game going again."

Rohit nodded. He didn't want doctor's advice at the moment.

"This place is ridiculous. How big is it?" Rohit had been in big, fancy houses before that were clearly out of his reach, but there was something familiar about Sanjay—his golf shirt, his pedestrian name—that prevented Rohit from discounting the house as the spoils of the rich.

Ram, who always seemed to know things, said, "Eight, nine thousand square feet maybe. I hear there's a home theater downstairs that seats twenty."

"And all from insurance?" Rohit asked.

"And family money," Ram said.

Urvashi, Ram's wife, leaned into the conversation. "Diamonds," she whispered.

Ram waved at his wife to be quiet. "It's hard to know where one income ends and the other begins. Most of the wives in this room will call him when their husbands have massive heart attacks. Well, they'll call me first. But then I can't do anything about a lifetime of ghee and stress."

Rohit's jaw tightened, in the way it did when someone cut him off on the freeway. Did everything come easy to Sanjay? Without food, the scotch had traveled quickly to his head. He'd been in the middle of the conversation but could no longer concentrate. All he heard were disjointed words. He didn't have the strength to join them together.

"I'm going to grab a bite to eat," he said to no one in particular and walked away. There were more people in the room now, some of whom had spilled onto the deck in the backyard. Rohit filled a plate with a large samosa and several pieces of boneless tandoori chicken. That Gayatri didn't want meat in their house annoyed him. They'd both grown up vegetarian, but her vegetarianism was strict and tied to religious things her mother believed. He took a bite of the chicken. It was hot, very moist, and spicy. He put more pieces on his plate and looked over at his group of friends. He liked them all very much, he decided. Then he carried his plate up the wide staircase and found a bathroom near the landing. He locked the door and sat on the edge of the bathtub. He finished the chicken and drank the scotch left in his glass in one swig.

There was no soap scum in the bathtub, the toilet was shining bright, and the countertop was clean. He opened the medicine cabinet: a full tube of Colgate, two new toothbrushes, and a couple of travel sticks of deodorant. He opened the drawers below the sink and found bottles of shampoo and conditioner, soap, toilet paper, tampons, and a stack of new, soft, white towels. The bathroom, the most intimate of spaces, without a hint of intimacy. Did Kamala forbid her kids from using it?

Rohit peed a bit in the toilet and then aimed toward the seat and beyond. He took some pleasure in missing the toilet altogether, creating little yellow puddles on the floor. After he thought he was done, he obsessively shook out the last drops.

He was going to leave the toilet as he'd sullied it, but at the last moment, he took out ample tissue and cleaned up his mess.

There was no one on the stairs or in the entryway, though the buzz of the party continued downstairs. Gayatri would have said it was rude to look around uninvited. He was never rude.

He walked down the hall, past several closed doors. He stopped to open one. A boy's room filled with toys. He kept walking down the hall. The master bedroom was at the end. While the rooms downstairs were ornate and full, this one was spare and perfect, reminding him of a magazine article he'd once read about a five-star Japanese hotel fitted in a similar simplicity.

There were large windows at one end of the room that looked onto a hillside of yellow rolling hills the color of a lion's back and filled with enormous, unruly oaks. Two brown-leather chairs were placed near the windows. He sat down on one of them and raised his feet on the ottoman. He'd always assumed roots needed flat land, but these oaks grew on a slope. He stood and went into the bathroom, where there was a bathtub the size of a small Jacuzzi. He stepped into it and sat down as if he were taking a bath. There was enough room for him and Gayatri to lie side by side. The only time he'd bathed with a woman was in college, in a tub much smaller than this. The bathing and the lovemaking had been too intimate. He wondered what she was up to now, whether she was married and had kids. Sometimes he wished he still knew her.

He got out of the tub and stuck his head in the walk-in closet. There were at least three hundred neatly stacked saris on one side and on the other side about thirty golf shirts, similar to the one Sanjay was wearing, all hung up, ironed, and arranged by color. He removed several of the dark shirts and replaced them among the light shirts. He ran a finger down one pile of Kamala's saris, then pushed his hands between them and felt the cool silk and the hard gold embroidery.

He walked out of the closet and laid down on the bed, which was low to the ground. After their fights, was Sanjay banished to another room? He tried picturing them making love on this bed, and his mind wandered over to Kamala. She was attractive and yet gave off no sexual energy.

On the night table, he noticed a watch that he then picked up. He considered Rolexes too flashy, but this one was classic: a metal band with a light gray-silver face. It was the type of watch certain men wore to quietly announce to those who knew how to notice that they had some money. He tapped at the crystal face with his finger and felt the weight. Then he stood and put the watch in his pocket. Before he left the room, he ran his hand over the bed to make it neat again.

Downstairs, he poured himself just a drop more of the scotch.

"Where have you been?" Gayatri asked when he returned. She and the others were talking to Sanjay and Kamala.

"I had to use the bathroom."

Rohit stole a glance at Sanjay's wrist. It was bare.

"This is a real stunning house," Rohit said, interrupting the conversation.

"Thank you," Kamala said. "I was just saying that we love it, but it doesn't hold the same place in our hearts as the little house on Sparrow Avenue."

"We had many hard times there," Sanjay said, and before he was finished taking a breath between clauses, Kamala finished his sentence. "But we also had some good times."

"Really? What kind of hard times?" Rohit kept his eyes on Kamala because he knew Gayatri was giving him a hard stare.

"Someone is chatty today," Gayatri said. She moved her hand toward Rohit's glass, but he moved it just out of her reach.

"I'm good," Rohit said, now looking straight at Gayatri.

"It's OK," Kamala said. "We'd left India mainly because Sanjay and his father were fighting. When we got here, we didn't know what we were going to do. Some of our friends had done well in the insurance business. We didn't even know what that was. In the beginning, Sanjay didn't have very many clients. There was just enough money to get by."

"I'm glad things have worked out," Rohit said. "This place really is amazing."

"Thank you," Sanjay said. "Please stay and enjoy. We should make our rounds."

"I'm ready to head home," Rohit said after the hosts had left.

"We've barely been here," Gayatri said.

Rohit went downstairs to collect his kids. A long table was filled with hot dogs, pizza, chips, and soft drinks. There were about twenty-five kids, some watching TV. The older boys were playing pool, and a few girls, including Neha, played Ping-Pong. *Tom and Jerry* was on the big screen.

Rohit announced to his kids that they were leaving.

"We just got here," Arvind said. "This place is so much fun."

"I know, but we need to go now," Rohit said impatiently.

Neha placed the Ping-Pong paddle and a ball on the table. "Come on, Arvind."

Upstairs, they found Sanjay had cornered Gayatri near the front door. "Please don't tell me you're leaving already. You've just gotten here. And there is so much more food."

"The kids have homework," Gayatri said.

"Just stay for a little bit more," Sanjay insisted.

"We have to get going," Rohit said too strongly.

As a way of showing his resolve to leave, he reached into his pocket for the keys. But the watch came out as well and fell to the marble floor, landing on its face.

Rohit bent to pick it up. It was undamaged.

"Nice watch," Sanjay said.

"It was pinching me a little," Rohit said, rubbing his wrist. He glanced at Gayatri, whose eyes settled on the watch. He put the watch on his wrist. It was, indeed, too tight.

Then he heard Sanjay's voice, the one he used with his clients when approaching the issue of life insurance. "Rohit. Can we talk for a moment?"

"I can't," Rohit said. "We need to get going."

"Don't worry. I'll keep it quick."

"Why don't you wait for me in the car?" he said to Gayatri.

Sanjay and Kamala had asked their interior designer to create a study with a sense of gravity and purpose. The desk in the middle of the room was large and heavy, an enormous slab of stone lowered and then finished with a walnut trim. Floor-to-ceiling built-in bookshelves on one wall were packed with hardcovers, first editions, and large, expensive art books.

"Have you read all of these?" Rohit asked.

Sanjay was leaning against the desk. He shook his head. "The designer bought books based on my tastes. Who has the time to read?"

"I don't know whether I've read a book in over a decade," Rohit said. He reached for the books, using both hands to touch them. He scanned the shelf. "Can you recommend something?"

"Let's talk about that another time. Can I see the watch?"

Rohit removed the watch from his wrist and handed it to him.

Sanjay quickly glanced at the face and then turned to the back. He read the inscription aloud for effect. "To Sanjay. With apologies." He looked up. "My father," he said.

"Touching," Rohit said.

Sanjay carefully placed the watch around his wrist to show how perfectly it fit. Then he removed it immediately, as if it had singed him, and placed it on the desk in front of Rohit.

"You know what, go ahead," Sanjay said, seeming agitated. "Take it. You can easily have it adjusted so that it fits your wrist."

Rohit looked at Sanjay, waiting for some signal that he was joking. The beginning of a smile, a shaking of the head. But there was nothing. Sanjay was serious.

"Every couple of mornings, I wind it up, thinking I'm going to wear it, but it just sits there and dies. I've never actually worn it for more than a few minutes."

Rohit looked at the watch.

"Please," Sanjay said. "Take it."

"I don't want it," Rohit replied. He picked up the watch, turned it over, and read the inscription again. He put it to his ear and heard the seconds hand tick. The rhythm was rapid and sharp. "I'm sorry," he said and held the watch out to Sanjay. "I don't know what came over me."

"A decent jeweler can easily remove the inscription," Sanjay said.

"Yeah?" Rohit fastened the watch around his wrist and let his arm hang to the side, glancing down to see how it would look on him. I can't, Rohit was about to say.

"It's a reissue of a model from the 1950s called The Bombay," Sanjay said. "A limited edition run for the Indian market. The originals had a gold face, but they've toned it down here."

Rohit looked at it again. "It is quite understated."

"An ideal blend of the old and new."

Sanjay looked cool in the way he'd been when they first arrived at the party.

That afternoon, Rohit got the mower out and, for half an hour, methodically went up and down his lawn, making sure not to miss a single blade. When he was done, he carefully trimmed the edges of the lawn and swept and collected the stray pieces of grass. He stood in the late-afternoon sun with the smell of the freshly cut grass deep in his nose. He then walked back into the house, got a glass of water from the kitchen, and drank it greedily. Through the kitchen window, he could see Gayatri in the backyard, still in her sari, trimming the thorny zucchini leaves with clippers and her bare hands. There was a neat pile of yellow zucchinis and tomatoes at the edge of the vegetable bed. Arvind was helping Gayatri by removing weeds from the bed, and Neha was at the far end of the yard, watering the roses.

Rohit walked out with a couple of bottles of water and handed one to Gayatri. As she took it, she noticed the watch on Rohit's wrist.

"Is everything OK?" she asked.

"I'm fine," Rohit said.

"You've been moody for months. You know, if we need to shut the site down, we'll figure something out. Your old job is solid work. And you're good at it. It's gotten us all this." She stood up, gestured toward the house, and then took a long sip of the water.

He looked at her in the bland sari. They had first played together as toddlers in India. When it was time to be married, his parents had suggested Gayatri. Though he had not seen her in over two decades, he still remembered her sweet smile. They had a stable marriage and were raising two good kids. She was still a beautiful woman, though, bathed in the orange light of dusk, wearing her party sari, her face filled with emotion, she looked like some kind of goddess of shame.

"It's not your watch," she said, whispering so Arvind wouldn't hear her.

Rohit cupped his hand around it. "I know. But I can't give it back now."

PART TWO

The Blind Writer

I. The Fall

When I was a graduate student, preparing for a career I would eventually abandon, I did something that, now that I am older and finely attuned to the cruelty of consequence, surprises me.

I received an email announcing that a prominent writer spending a year at the Center—a think tank of sorts at my university where established writers and scholars came for a year to think—needed an assistant. Over the years, these stays had produced many scholarly books that I read then with the care and precision of a miniaturist but are now just books in stacked, weakened boxes in a garage we once thought was spacious. There was no name attached to the writer in the email, but the assigned duties—reading to him from the newspaper, transcribing notes he'd spoken into a recorder—confirmed a rumor I'd heard that Anil Trivedi, the great blind Indian writer, was at the Center for the year. The list of occupants of the Center was a guarded secret, to ensure that they would not have admirers dropping in.

At first, I sat on the email, assuming that someone more qualified (to read the paper to a blind man!) would contact him. Had it been someone whose books I loved—a mute Roth, a paraplegic García Márquez, even a late-cancer Carver—I would have jumped at the opportunity. And yet Trivedi's books had been very important to me, though I wouldn't readily admit this in front of my fellow students, who were all obsessed with falling off a cutting edge. His straightforward prose had made the stories of my extended family feel literary.

When another email went out, this time with the added detail that the pay rate was fifteen dollars an hour, I picked up the phone. I wanted to be physically close to a writer, as if proximity would make my ambitions real. And the idea of riding my Schwinn every couple of days into the hills above the campus to read to a blind man had the whiff of romance I'd expected from graduate school. In the year I had been there, it had just been numbing seminars on topics that sounded good on paper—"The Short, Happy Life of the Enlightenment," "The Sexual Politics of the American Reconstruction"—but turned out to be failures. I'd wanted to fall in love with a graduate student in English, busty, studious, a lover of me and the modernists, and instead I'd ended up with a few bad dates with an econ postdoc working on a project on microlending.

A woman picked up the phone.

"I am calling about the assistant job."

"Why else would you call?"

She didn't let me answer.

"Are you a student?"

"Graduate."

"He doesn't want graduate students in English."

"I'm in history."

"I'm sure you are."

Were these attempts at humor?

She gave me directions to their place and told me to come that afternoon at four. I had a car, my father's old, beige Taurus that he had left for me when he moved to New York, but I rode my bike.

It was late afternoon, the middle of a warm California fall, and I was riding through the tree-lined streets, ushered along by a slight tailwind. This was the luxury of being twenty-four, living in a temperate place, with a scholarship that was just generous enough to let me finally buy bottles of Anchor Steam instead of cans of Keystone.

I rode through campus and into blocks and blocks of small Craftsman bungalows, rambling Victorians, and old Spanish adobes that populated the faculty ghetto. The size of a faculty member's house was roughly equivalent to the department he or she occupied. The medical and law faculty, and the local moguls who chose to live close to campus, had multiple stories, while the humanists and social scientists had to make do with one, unless they'd had a textbook or a novel that had done particularly well, or they had family money they were tired of hiding.

The house was a small, one-story bungalow covered by the afternoon shadow of a much-larger main house.

I knocked on the door and took two steps back. The woman on the phone hadn't mentioned it, but I had assumed she was the writer's wife.

She opened the door, and there standing in front of me was a woman—and I know this is an absurd, beaten-down phrase—who took my breath away. She was in her mid-thirties, and in her well-pressed purple salwar-kameez, she tapped into that part of me that had always wanted, at some core level, an ideal of Hindu womanhood: devoted, doting, pure, and beautiful. But beneath the long shirt was a woman with a body that reminded me of the full figures in the *Playboys* I'd teethed on during puberty. I imagined the wife as the mythical Sita in tasteful topless shots, a scarf casually covering the mound below.

Of course she'd married a blind man. She blinded the seeing. It seemed that successful blind men always had younger, attractive wives who believed their men saw only their inner beauty.

"It's not polite to stare," said a voice coming from behind the wife.

"Anil," Mira chided. "Let's not chase him away before he's even stepped in the door."

I had been staring. Any man who didn't was just too afraid to look.

"Come in," Mira said.

Later I would learn that Anil had wanted a female assistant, but Mira had insisted on a man so that she could leave them alone and not have to worry.

"He knows I'm just playing with him," Anil said. "We already have good taste in women in common."

I walked into the living room, following Mira, and introduced myself.

Anil and Mira were housed in a cottage in the back of a large house owned by a very wealthy white couple who had a thing for India and the arts. They offered the cottage free of charge to the Center in exchange for getting the visiting writers and, in the best of circumstances, Indian writers.

The cottage was Indian themed—with Gujarati tapestries and Mughal miniatures on the walls, bronze sculptures of Ganesh and the Buddha on small pedestals, and Kashmiri rugs on the floor, scattered below modern furniture by well-known designers, many of whom also had some connection to India themselves.

Sitting comfortably in a black Eames chair, Anil was even slighter than I had pictured in my mind. He had a long, thin neck and a round head that made him look like a tortoise. His clothes were meticulous—light-gray gabardine slacks without pleats, a crisp white shirt, a dark-green button-down cashmere sweater, and soft Cole Haan loafers. He was not dressed for the California fall. I'd expected him to be wearing sunglasses, but he wasn't. His eyelids were halfway closed, and I could see his eyes moving below them. I'd assumed he was completely blind, but right then I wasn't sure. I didn't feel free to stare at his wife.

"Sit down," he said signaling with two fingers. "What can Mira get you?"

"I'm fine, thank you," I said, not wanting to put them out.

"You have to have something," Anil insisted, in that Old World way where offering something to a guest, and having a woman take care of it, was reflex.

"Tea?" I ventured.

"Tea it is," Anil said.

Mira walked out of the room. As one source of my nerves left, I remembered the other. I was, after all, sitting in front of a writer, who in certain circles was much beloved. From what I had read of his work, there was a great distance between the man described in words and paragraphs and the shrunken, fine-boned man sitting in front of me. The real thing always disappoints.

"So why are you here, Rakesh?" Anil asked.

This was not that complicated a question.

I was born in India, and after brief stops in London and Toronto, I had grown up in San Francisco, the only child of a mother and father who'd stopped feeling much for each other even before I was born. Or to be more exacting, my mother felt nothing for my father, who then surrendered to the emotional absence in the marriage. Though they thought it would, my birth and our transcontinental move several years later changed nothing in how my mother felt. In San Francisco, I learned to ride a bike on a thin strip of sidewalk in front of our apartment building and walked to and from the local elementary school by myself.

I graduated from my high school third in a class of five hundred. I was at the top of my class through the middle of my senior year, and knowing I would stay there, I flinched and slacked off a bit. I was afraid, not only of winning this particular horse race but, as I learned later, of winning in general. I played on my high school tennis team and won quite a few matches over the years. But in the matches that really mattered, I would speed ahead and then lose focus and fall in three sets. I was always concerned about how my opponent would feel after losing.

I traveled across the bay to Berkeley for college, took the economics classes I was supposed to, and did my summer internships in brokerage offices in San Francisco's financial district. But quietly, I fed my ambition to be a writer. I took fiction-writing classes and earned consistent, sometimes effusive praise, particularly for a story I wrote about a college student who tries committing suicide by hanging himself from a magnolia tree in his parents' front yard but ends up alive and not so well, with a broken leg, when the branch gives out. I wrote for the college paper, starting off covering track and women's soccer and working my way up to sports editor. I ended up double majoring in economics and history. I'd started off college wanting to be a journalist but then decided later to be a historian. Both professions, in my eye, were centered on investigating sources and connecting the dots. I chose history because it was the closest thing to English.

The spring semester of my senior year, my economics degree earned me a great job in finance, but I decided instead to go into a graduate program in history, to which I had secretly applied the previous fall. What I really wanted to do was write, but I couldn't say that to my parents, who'd worked very hard to pay for my college. My father wasn't pleased about my graduate-school decision, but I made him feel better when I told him that Stanford had awarded me a full, generous scholarship.

"Wall Street will always be there," I had foolishly said. I wish my father had slapped me and said, "No it won't. Opportunity has a short shelf life."

I had been taking my history seminars for the past year and writing fiction in the evenings. In college, the stories seemed to arrive in paragraphs and pages every time I sat down at my desk. Now, the words came, but the confidence and crispness of the language was gone. I was overwriting.

And then the email came. I was there, to answer Anil's question, because being close to a real-life writer meant being close to a literary writing life I desperately wanted but was too scared to openly admit. In the few minutes I had been there, I realized that this was precisely the life I wanted: a beautiful wife, itinerant travel, and a solid reputation to rest my feet on when I reached my sixties.

"I need the money," I said.

"Rakesh what?"

"Mehta."

"A businessman. You must be Gujarati."

I didn't respond. Why had I made this out to be about money? I didn't want to seem like a sycophant. But now I just sounded like a guy who was looking to make an extra buck. Though given the choice, I preferred the perception that this was about money over some strange desire for literary osmosis.

"C'mon. Stereotypes are a perfect way to break the ice."

"Don't worry," I said. "As a rule, I don't get offended."

"Really?"

"Life is offensive enough already. I'd be exhausted if I constantly got offended at things."

"That's awfully dark for someone so young."

I was lost within the conversation, saying things I didn't mean, coming off as someone I wasn't.

"Well, of course, it's not just the money," I finally said. "It's nice to spend time with you."

"Trust me. Spending time with me is not that exciting."

I smiled and nodded my head to convey that he was just being modest. I forgot he couldn't see this gesture, and that I had stayed silent when it was my turn to talk.

"Mira says you are a young historian. What is your research on?"

I hated the question. I'd always hated the question. For a while, I said I didn't know. But then I decided that I should and that if I really had no clue, I had no business being there.

Just then, Mira walked back into the room with a tea serving. I kept my eyes away from her until I got the next sentence out. "I'm just taking classes right now. I'm interested in the early British East India Company in Surat, but I don't know anything beyond that."

"It's good not to know where you're going sometimes. It keeps you open to possibility."

For a few minutes, we sugared and drank the tea. Strong, milky tea, close to the best I had tasted from Bombay tea stalls and from my mother's kitchen.

Anil needed me three days a week, in the morning from eight to eleven. "Depending on your time and my needs, we can increase the days if things work out."

"Do you need to check my references?" I asked.

"So they can tell me that you can read?"

"You'll let a stranger into your house without checking up on him?"

"Do you have any violent tendencies?"

"Not that I know of."

"What do you think, Mira? Can you handle a young, handsome man in our midst?"

Mira looked straight at me and then slowly scanned me over, barely moving her head. I broke out into a little sweat all along my back and felt the initial leanings of an erection.

"He seems safe enough," Mira said.

I felt like a child being toyed with by knowing adults.

We finished the tea, and I got up to leave. My first day was the following morning.

"Plan to eat with us. I like the paper with my breakfast."

"I'll walk you out," Mira said.

"Don't worry. I'll be fine."

I ran out before she could get any closer.

After meeting Anil and Mira, I rode straight to the library, checked out all of Anil's books, and organized them chronologically in my cubicle. The more recent looked as though they had never been checked out, and the older ones still needed the new checkout barcodes that had been implemented a decade before. He'd written fifteen books of fiction, memoir, and social and family history. And while the books themselves were works of sharp observation, with occasional moments of comedy and aesthetic flourish, they now had a limited audience. His current fame rested largely on the fact that despite his blindness, he'd written so many books. The critics were amazed at the feat but ultimately treated it as an elaborate parlor trick, rather than the sustained literary production that it was. A seeing writer with fifteen books meant a consistent career. But for Trivedi, the impressive stamina of being a writer—the willingness to get up day after day, year after year, and return to the cruelty of a desk—was always outplayed by his blindness.

As I remembered by quickly flipping through his earliest book, Anil had been blind since he was six months old. He was born with sight, and just as his eyes picked up speed and he began to recognize the shapes in front of him, a rare degenerative disease set in. He'd not had the time to store images he could look back to as his life progressed.

In this first book, I kept expecting the anger to arrive, but what I read instead was a work of nostalgia about a very happy childhood. Details about his blindness were scant and almost dismissive. Much of the first half of the book was about how he had been able to do everything that seeing children could do. The success of the book seemed to be in painting a portrait of a comfortable, happy childhood spent in a country home, constantly buzzing with family, friends, and servants.

When he was sixteen, Anil had traveled to Georgia, to a well-known school for the blind in Atlanta. The curriculum included learning Braille and traditional topics such as history and English. But the headmaster was a Booker T. type who thought that what his boys needed to learn first and foremost was how to operate in the world—walking down the street like the seeing, buying cold medicine from the drug store, accepting help, navigating Jim Crow. At the school, among young, blind blacks, Anil learned that the world was shit, and the only way to not step in it was a careful balance between charm and smarts. Anil arrived as a fattened, feted first child and left sinewy, with a taste for women and a dangerous outward confidence. He'd lost his virginity between the confused legs of a young woman named Shira from the sister blind school for girls. He vowed after that fumbling mess that he would never be with a blind woman again.

Anil was known primarily as a memoirist, in the tradition of the great memoirists who came out of the generation before him—Gandhi, Nehru, and Nirad Chaudhuri. His life did not have the public intrigue that made Gandhi's and Nehru's books interesting, nor had he done the broad reading that made Chaudhuri's books so long. But blindness was his thing, the lens through which he saw everything. It elongated moments that were either brief or didn't warrant mention for the seeing. The mundane suddenly had tension. Even in the hands of a master of detail like Flaubert, long passages on learning how to ride a bike would eventually fall flat, but with Anil, the particulars about getting on a bike for the first time were thrilling. I felt a great sense of accomplishment when he finally rode around the family compound all on his own. It was participatory writing.

The publishers were banking on the fact that the novelty of a blind man's memoir was enough to move product. And it was. The success of that first book—in the United States, England, and India—had allowed Anil to write other books about the lives of his parents and grandparents under the British Raj. His paternal grandfather had made a fortune in the import of cotton during the American Civil War, when American cotton production had taken a nosedive. And that windfall had financially set up the family for the generations that followed, though there was less and less as the years went by. Anil grew up comfortably, but he had to work some if he wanted to continue to have comfort into adult life.

It was one of the later books that I was most interested in reading. *Blind Lust*. But I didn't like reading out of order, and so I had to wait until I had skimmed through most of the early ones. There weren't many skills I'd gained as a graduate student, but I'd become highly proficient at knowing where to find the heart of a book and to skip the rest.

The dedication: "For my love, wherever I may find her."

From the first page, *Blind Lust* had something the others didn't. It delved into the muck of Anil's inner life. The first line hooked me. "As the blind son of a wealthy Indian family, I found my greatest solace from the darkness when I was alone, masturbating."

In those first few pages, Anil described the unique challenge of beating off in an enormous house where privacy had no currency. The large, rambling rooms were *loosely* partitioned by nuclear family. Anil's grandparents, their four children, and all of their children lived in the house. Sixteen people spread through ten thousand square feet of high-ceilinged rooms and long breezeways. Since the day it had been completed, the house had never been completely empty. Kids and servants and cooks spilled out of every corner. The first challenge was in finding a quiet place where no one would intrude.

After some searching, Anil found a place in the basement, in a cool corner where a year's worth of rice and wheat were stored in large, four-foot-high vats. Anil lay down behind them, and if anyone walked into the basement, he would remain hidden. He came down there five, six times a week.

What followed in the book was a minute detailing of every sexual experience Anil had had until he reached the age of fifty.

His mother had assumed asexuality in her son. And so she thought nothing of the fact that a new servant—an eighteen-year-old girl—was given the responsibility in the mornings of helping a teenage Anil bathe and get dressed. For years, an older servant had done the work, but she'd broken her hip recently and could no longer do the job. Anil had been having erections in the bath for some time, but the old woman had stopped noticing; and later as her eyes went bad, she saw nothing. But when the younger servant took over the work, things changed. For the first couple of days, the girl pretended she didn't see. But by the third day, she herself couldn't turn away. "I didn't know it then," Anil wrote in language that was both formal and playful, "but I had quite a large penis, which would prove to be unmanageable to some later in my life. But that morning, the servant girl—I think her name was Savita—had no problem with it." When her hand grazed him, Anil let out an enormous breath. And from that morning on, Anil would take his warm bath, and somewhere in the middle, Savita would soap his body, use her hands, and then wash him off with fresh hot water. Anil acknowledged that initiating his sexual life at the hands of a servant might not have been the healthiest of beginnings.

Along with sexual frankness, there was, finally, the anger I had expected.

His parents knew better, but they couldn't stop babying him. And with so much babying, Anil arrived at his sixteenth birthday pudgy, insolent, and ultimately, angry. He did nothing himself, and when his mother said so, his reply shut her down.

"You're the one who's insisted that I do nothing. Now that I've settled into that role, you want me to be self-sufficient?"

His mother could have said yes, but her guilt overwhelmed her and she continued bringing him his meals. The doctors had identified the disease that took Anil's sight, but his mother was God fearing and assumed her actions had somehow started the chain reaction that culminated in Anil's blindness. Anil knew this and had his mother and the rest of the family on the hook.

Anil's uncle, his father's brother, arrived for a visit and was disgusted with the power Anil had over the household. The uncle had recently moved to Atlanta to take over the psychiatry department of the city's largest hospital and had met the headmaster of the local school for the colored blind. As a psychiatrist, the uncle was all about recognizing and saying the truth.

"I'll take Anil back with me," the uncle insisted. "He'll die from sugar and anger if we leave him here."

Anil's parents were hesitant, and Anil himself didn't want to go. What fool would want to leave this situation? But the uncle insisted that he would accompany him every step of the way and that he'd be right there in town if he ever needed anything. The uncle waited to reach Atlanta before telling Anil that he was leaving in another month to take up a better post in San Francisco.

"You lied to my parents," Anil said.

"I did. I promise you'll thank me for it."

In Georgia, after Anil had been at the school for two years, he and three of his classmates were driven, by the headmaster, to a whorehouse in the backcountry as a reward for being at the top of their class. The headmaster sat in the parlor with the madam, smoking menthols and drinking syrupy vermouth on ice, while the boys lost their senses.

Rose was busty and, like her namesake, smelled of day-old flowers. Anil came in twenty seconds after he was finally in her, but she massaged his head and back and let him stay long enough to try again. "I've always had a soft spot in my heart for whores," Anil wrote. "There had been the blind girl Shira before this, but I considered Rose my first."

Anil had planned to go back home after high school, but he was encouraged by a school counselor to apply to American colleges. He won a good scholarship to Berkeley, and what it didn't cover was covered by his uncle, who was now getting wealthy in private practice in San Francisco.

I had not been looking for a father figure when I took the reading job. But knowing that Anil had gone to Berkeley, more than the fact that we were Indians of the same caste, made me now feel tied to him in a special way. Though I had moved across the bay for graduate school, I had remained loyal to the sprawling campus of my college years. With Anil, I felt a sense of the continuity that sons must feel when they attend their father's alma mater. Generations at Yale or Princeton—a type of American aristocracy of assumed merit. We weren't going to talk about the yearly disappointments of Cal football, but it was nice to imagine him sitting for lecture in Wheeler Hall decades before me. I had a close relationship with my father in so many ways, but not when it came to school ties and the sense of belonging and faith in possibility they engendered. I saw him as a high-level worker and saw myself ascending to a different class populated by Anils and Miras.

At Berkeley, Anil attracted several women, all of whom came from nice families, dressed conservatively for class, and had fought hard with their stern, drunk fathers to let them go to Berkeley. They weren't adventurous enough to openly oppose the war in Vietnam or drop acid, but in Anil, they found a safe way to step out of their lives. Each of them cared for him, walked him to and from class, asked about India, divulged their fatigue with Catholic dogma about sex. This last bit of information would seem like an ideal segue to taking their relationship to a new place, but they all backed away.

"For the whole time I was getting rejected, I thought they were scared of intimacy with an injured man. And they were, but I had misread the nature of the injury. They were happy to be seen walking around with me, and taking care of me, but that was it. In those days, and still today, I am as unthreatening as a colored man gets."

Anil majored in English and, for his senior project, wrote the first two chapters of what would become his first book. A year after he graduated Berkeley, the memoir came out to strong reviews and brisk sales. The period of women unwilling to have sex with him came to a decisive end.

Through his twenties and thirties, after he'd moved to Manhattan, there were a string of women. From his descriptions, they were the beauties at a party, the lonely ones no one was brave enough to approach. Anil was always the center of attention, the writer with the popular memoirs that sold well among lawyers and psychiatrists on the Upper East Side and homesteading mothers in Humboldt County.

Anil loved having sex with women, and they loved him, for being blind, for not looking at them when they didn't want to be looked at. Some stayed for a night or a week; others stayed for longer, becoming his confidant, secretary, and eyes. But Anil sensed that there was a limit to what they could give and what he could give in return, and that limit was reached somewhere around the two-year mark.

Later, he'd hear from mutual friends that the women had moved to a house in Westchester and were expecting, even though they'd insisted to him that marriage and kids were not right for them. Not after what they'd realized about themselves in the sixties.

The sensation of reading about Anil's sexual conquests was a strange one. In one way, it was soft porn, and that kept me turning page after page as I sat there in the strangely erotic place that is a dimly lit, far corner of a research library, late into the night. But there was something missing in the descriptions. He talked about the women and how he felt, but inevitably there were no clear descriptions of what these women looked and felt like during sex. There was plenty of detail in describing other aspects of his life. In the earlier books, he had painstakingly gone through the process of describing the layout of the family house and the large compound. I could visualize everything. But here, a woman was "busty"; her vagina was "wet." Weak stuff. Perhaps he was being coy. He didn't seem to have an eye for detail where it mattered most. The descriptions were, ultimately, solipsistic. I got to know a lot about him at the coital moment, but I desperately wanted some of her and her and her.

Ultimately, the book was deeply sad. There was all the sex, but at the end, there was a lonely man, living well on his fame, now fattened from his own checkbook. "I have spent my life looking inside the women I have loved, digging below the surface; not one has returned the kindness."

I am not one to get lost in a book, to lose track of time, to forget to eat a meal. But there was a voice over the loud speaker, announcing that the library would close in fifteen minutes. I had sat for five straight hours. As I walked toward the library exit, with blurred images of Anil's women in my mind, I had one question. Who was the Mira I'd met earlier that day? Another two-year stop? I feared that Anil had finally found the woman he had been waiting for. And if this was the case, that made two of us.

When I arrived that first morning, still a little sleepy from my late night, Anil was sitting in the living room, drinking a cup of tea.

"One hundred years old," he said, holding up a delicate teacup with a thin paisley pattern. "From the collection of the Maharaja of Gwalior. They insist we use them." He pointed to the main house outside. "It's a little absurd, but they want us to live with the art."

Anil was addicted to caffeine and liked the taste of Mira's sugary tea, which reminded him of his mother. He'd read that Balzac drank cups and cups of coffee. Early in his writing life, Anil had tried to be a writer by imitating writerly ways—he ordered stationery with his name on top, he bought an expensive fountain pen that he asked his transcribers to use, he worked early in the morning and then late into the night. Out of all these habits, it was the caffeine that had stuck, bits of it dripping into his body throughout the day.

There was nothing about Anil's current physical being that suggested he was the protagonist of *Blind Lust*. I would have thought it was all an elaborate, frat-boy boast, were it not for Mira. Whatever power he had to attract beautiful women had culminated in her.

I sat down, and Anil leaned over and poured me a cup of tea from a buffed, silver teapot. He felt around for the cup, but once he located it, he poured with precision—the right amount of liquid, from an ideal height, with no misplaced drops. I took the cup and saucer in my hands, and instantly my right hand started shaking.

"Maybe I should just go get a mug from the kitchen," I said.

"Suit yourself," Anil said. "Somehow the tea tastes much better when you drink it from these cups."

As if demonstrating the sensual arts, Anil brought the cup to his mouth, took a slow inhale of the cardamom, let his lower lip rest on the rim for a second, and then tipped the cup slightly to let the hot liquid graze his tongue, pour down his throat, and warm his heart.

I gave it a try.

"What do you think?"

There was something about the porcelain that made the tea taste closer to nectar rather than a simple source of caffeine. I had some sense of why everyone was looking to drink from a holy grail.

"How am I ever going to go back to a cheap tea mug?"

"I don't think you can," Anil said. "You'll just have to steal one of these when I'm not looking."

I thought he was making a joke, but he just moved on and gestured to the papers in front of him. I took another sip of the tea and tried to get a look at his eyes.

My first introduction to blindness was through comic books. Much of my religious and moral education came from the *Amar Chitra Katha,* Indian comics my parents bought for me when we were coming to America. It gave me something to do on the long plane ride over, and it filled me with Indian religious and cultural lessons just as I was arriving in a place with an entirely new set of rules. Most of the comics were religious stories from the *Ramayana* and *Mahabharat,* while others were morality tales on how to be a good child, the rules of marriage, and the importance of honesty. The more I think I about it, the more I realize that my parents just wanted to keep me—then, an exhausting, hyper eight-year-old—occupied for the plane ride, and anything else that stuck was gravy.

For all these years, one particular comic had burrowed deep into my mind. The details of how the story starts and ends are now not very clear, but I have an image of a son and his blind parents, whom he dutifully takes care of, at the cost of living his own life. They insist that they don't need much care, but it's clear that they can't do a thing without his help. They spend their days going from village to village, earning admiration for the son and being fed meals of rice and lentils. At one point, the father grows too weak to walk, and so the son constructs a simple, wooden contraption, similar to a baby backpack, and carries him on his back.

As a child, I understood the lesson of filial piety. But I kept reading the comic over and over again for its horror value. The blind parents—the father's eyes somehow permanently sealed shut with the type of stitching found on old footballs, the mother's eyes open, gray, and unseeing—were monstrous, and their predicament was a state I thought worse than death. I couldn't keep my eyes away.

Since then, I had seen Ray Charles and Stevie Wonder on TV and passed blind people on the street with their sticks, but Anil was the first time I interacted with an actual blind man. And right then, at the beginning of what I now think of as a mentorship, his eyes were a little unsettling.

Sitting on the coffee table in between us was a stack of newspapers—the *New York Times, Financial Times,* the *Washington Post,* the *Times of India,* the *Hindu.* And then another stack of magazines—the *Economist,* the *New Yorker,* the *New York Review of Books, GQ.*

"How shall we start?" I asked. Reading to a literary blind man seemed at once the easiest and hardest job in the world.

"*We* are not starting anything. You are."

Both he and Mira shared this similar abrasiveness that they mistook for humor. It made me realize that as familiar as they and the cooking smells in the house seemed, I didn't know them at all.

"Just start going over the headlines and the first paragraphs of each story, and I'll tell you to read on or skip to the next thing."

"Any paper in particular?"

I waited for a few seconds, but Anil didn't answer. I picked up the *New York Times* and started reading from above the fold. Anil leaned back on the couch and seemed to close his eyes, though physically I couldn't tell the difference between when they were open and when they weren't. He'd eased up on a certain retinal alertness and transferred the work to his ears.

Over the next two hours, I got through only two newspapers— the *New York Times* and the *Times of India*. With each section, I started in the front and went through page after page. For every five headlines, I read through one article, usually stopping around the halfway mark, when Anil raised his hand slightly. At the end of the two hours, I felt the type of exhaustion I felt after my first quarter in graduate school, when I spent every spare moment of the day preparing for class, reading pages and pages of Marx, who should have made more sense than he did. That morning, my mind was not exhausted, but my jaw, mouth, and eyes were all in need of rest. Reading in silence swallowed up mistakes. Reading aloud made me realize just how difficult it was to read consistently—to pronounce words I had never actually said aloud correctly, to enunciate. If there was something I didn't understand when I was reading to myself, I could fool myself into thinking I did. With Anil, there was always a moment when he would stop and ask me to discuss what I'd just read. I didn't want to be caught being the blind reader who read but did not comprehend.

I was about to pick up another paper when Anil turned to me: "Are you happy?"

"Of course," I said without letting a second pass.

"Not with sitting here reading the paper to me. I mean really happy. It's a question I like to ask. If we're going to spend time together, I want to know with whom I'm spending it."

Suddenly, I got nervous. I felt like I was being tested, not necessarily about the extent of my happiness but about how I was going to approach this difficult question. I'd never been good at logic puzzles and hard questions that require instant answers.

"I suppose I am," I said.

I couldn't have known then that even if I wasn't perfectly happy, I was walking around bathed in a layer of gold dust. I could do whatever I wanted, whenever I wanted, on a campus filled with palm trees. Is there an age packed with more possibility and promise than twenty-four?

"You suppose?"

"I am," I said. I was suddenly having trouble articulating the details of this happiness. Rattling off a list of *things* seemed shallow and imprecise. "A great university is paying me to read and write. On a whim, if I wanted to read everything Chekhov ever wrote, I could hole myself up in the library for days, and no one would say anything. I ride my bike everywhere. And on Thursdays after class, I go to the farmers' market and buy freshly grown peaches and flirt with the pretty hippy girls selling them."

"That sounds wonderful. But why is all this happiness?"

I thought about it for a moment. "I enjoy the freedom."

Anil looked at me and mulled over what I'd said as if he were an anthropologist and I'd just gotten done telling him about my peculiar mating habits.

"Are you?" I asked.

"Am I what?"

I hadn't meant it as a retort, but Anil didn't seem like he was accustomed to people throwing the question back at him. He didn't say anything for a full minute.

"I suppose you need to know who you're spending time with as well."

And then he let another minute pass.

"I think I am. More than I've ever been."

I couldn't understand how he couldn't be happy. The books, the beautiful wife. There was the issue of the eyesight, but he'd had enough time to work through that.

"There are the books and now the beautiful wife," he said, as if he had just read my mind. "But then again, it's such an absurd question. Since when did happiness become the point in life?"

Before I could respond, he moved on.

"Do you have a girlfriend?"

I was surprised by the question. My parents never asked me about girlfriends. They were aware of the word and the concept, but they steered clear of it. It was assumed that if I had them, I would stay quiet about it and then only introduce a girl when I was ready to marry her.

"I don't. Not at the moment."

I'd had girlfriends before, but no one who left a real mark until Helen. She and I had come into graduate school together. Her Yale degree intimidated me, but it was also a source of attraction. After class, we would linger. At department functions, we sat in the same corner, drank the free wine, and gossiped about the faculty and the other students. We looked for each other in the library. Somehow I knew that we were headed straight to each other, me the small asteroid, she the blazing sun.

That first Thanksgiving, she roasted a chicken for the few of us who had nowhere to go. After several bottles of wine, it was just the two of us in her small on-campus apartment. Her housemate was gone. The other guests had stumbled home. Outside, there was the beginning of the first of the rain.

"You know I'm seeing someone back home," she said, leaning in close to me. I could smell the wine and feel the warmth of her breath. "We've been together since our freshman year in college."

In one swift moment, my heart filled with blood and then split right in two.

For the previous several weeks, I'd let myself believe that Helen was going to be the one to get me through graduate school and beyond. I'd pictured her—down to the dark-blond curls, the fancy degree, and the easy sharpness—when I decided on graduate school. My perception of Wall Street women—pantsuits and ponytails—didn't have the same appeal.

"That's too bad," I said.

"It is," she responded and then leaned in to kiss me.

In college, I might have been more black-and-white about this situation; but this time I too leaned forward, and within minutes, she had stripped off every bit of my clothing, while remaining fully dressed herself. She seemed to like this arrangement. When I finally got her clothes off, her breasts filled my hands. Despite her protests, I insisted we keep a small light on so that I could see every part of her. We slept the next day until noon.

For the next few months, we met secretly, which made it all the more exciting. We would spend long afternoons in her second-floor apartment, our lovemaking miraculous in a way I had never experienced it before. And after, we would read, she going through lots of Yeats, Joyce, and the Irish nationalist movement, me working through Indian historiography. One afternoon, when I was reading a work on the Indian Ocean trade of the fifteenth century, with the book perched on her pale bottom for effect, I was the happiest I had ever been.

Finally, I brought up the conversation we'd been avoiding. I wanted to be out in the world with her, eating at restaurants and kissing her in daylight. I'd had enough of the hiding. A few of the friends she'd made since arriving at graduate school knew of the boyfriend back home, and so she had wanted to keep things with me a little quiet.

"I really like what we have here," I said. "And I'm assuming you don't have the same with that guy."

For some reason, she took offense at this suggestion.

"What he and I have is different," she said.

I didn't like the idea of some better life.

"And I love him," she added, perhaps because she felt guilty for cheating on him.

"Enough to still go down on me in a field?"

I knew I shouldn't have said this, but I was hurt.

"Fuck you," she said and walked out of her own apartment.

And that was it. Just that quickly, she cut me off. We were cordial at department functions, and while before I seemed to see her everywhere on campus, I no longer saw her. By the time the next school year started, she didn't return, deciding to stay home in New York.

I couldn't tell Anil this story, not yet at least.

"I did have one when I first started graduate school, but it has been quiet since. A few disastrous dates here and there."

"We'll have to find you a new girl then," Anil said. "That will make you even happier, at least temporarily."

I was still trying to figure out how to really answer his question about happiness, but he looked down at the papers and asked me to read him the *Times* sports page, which I had skipped.

Anil wasn't that interested in sports, but he was a huge baseball fan. Before television, Anil explained, Americans listened to ball games on the radio. It forced listeners to imagine what was happening on the field. When he was at home in New York, he often passed the humid summer evenings listening to games and recording ideas for work into a tape recorder. He loved the Mets over the Yankees. Then, I didn't know what that meant. And I still don't really understand the implications of the choice.

"It takes no courage to like the Yankees," Anil said when I asked. "Especially these days."

The baseball playoffs were under way, and both the Yankees and the Mets were in the mix. One of the stories was about the possibility of a Subway Series.

"Pedro belongs in Flushing," Anil said. "If he were there already, we'd certainly win it all this year."

I had no idea what that meant but felt that I should and nodded in assent.

"I think that's enough for today," Anil said. "Do you think this is something you might like doing?"

I had liked being around him and wanted more time to talk about books and writing. And I wanted to see Mira again, whom I expected to see during the time I was there but hadn't.

"Absolutely," I said, trying not to sound too eager.

"I'll see you tomorrow then."

He reached out his hand, and I shook it. His hand was large, and the handshake was firm, perhaps the remnant of a time when the rest of his body was strong as well.

For the first two weeks, I came in three times a week and stayed for two, sometimes three, hours a day. During that first week, I sat there and read to him, and in between newspaper stories, I nervously glanced at the beautiful objects of art and furniture around the house and at Anil. So much of this was new to me. After that first day when we'd talked about happiness and girlfriends, I'd expected that we would drink our tea and, for a couple of hours, meander between reading and lively conversations. He'd tell me stories about long dinners with famous authors and give me bits of advice on the writing life, and I would throw in a thing or two about my childhood. But by the second morning, Anil had retracted into a shell and just sat there, listening and nodding. It was as if he'd revealed too much the previous day, and now he needed to repent by going silent.

I got accustomed to the reading and was able to understand the little signs from Anil—the sounds he made, the way he turned his head—that marked when he wanted me to keep reading and when he wanted me to stop. Silence was a marker of interest. There were sections he liked—the front page, the international scene, the business page, and the arts section.

He had me read reviews of books written by people he did not know. I didn't ask any questions; I stuck to my job. Later, he told me that reading the reviews for people he knew was bad either way. A good review made him envious; a bad one he felt deeply, as though the review had been written about one of his own books.

By the end of that first week, I feared that I was failing in my duties. My reading was fine, but I assumed that he wanted something more in a reader, perhaps the type of witty repartee I just couldn't muster.

"That was a good first week," Anil said. "My instincts about your reading skills were spot-on. Have a great weekend, and I'll see you back here next week."

I laughed weakly. He handed me an envelope with my wages, which reminded me that I was, after all, hired help. As I rode away on my bike, I felt flat and a little depressed. That night, I blew the money on several rounds of drinks with friends.

Early the following week, I was drinking my tea and flipping through a magazine while Anil was using the restroom.

"What are you reading?" he asked when he came back and sat down.

"*GQ*," I said.

"Anything good?"

At first, I didn't want to mention that I'd lingered on a black-and-white spread of the model Cindy Crawford in various modes of undress. I didn't want to like her, and her perfect body, and that mole, and those tanned long legs. Everybody was having a Cindy Crawford moment, and I didn't want to be so typical.

"An article on the perfect wingtip. Interested?"

"Never been much of a fan. Too much going on."

"Cindy Crawford," I ventured. I assumed he didn't know who she was.

"Ah," he said. "That's what those magazines are really good for. Let me see."

He pointed to a space on the coffee table in front of him, and I placed the magazine there, open to a spread of her wearing just a men's white dress shirt. He quietly ran his hand across the photographs and then tapped his fingers all over her body as if he were lightly pressing down on the keys of a piano.

"Nice woman," he said. "I met her at a party once. She said she loved my work. I told her I loved her body of work as well."

He started laughing at this memory.

"Did you really say that?"

"I did. And she thanked me earnestly. She was a little surprised that I knew of her."

Anil closed the magazine, pushed it back toward me, and then quietly said beneath his breath, "women."

"They are complicated," I said to keep the conversation going.

"For a while, they can be so perfect. The better ones remain perfect."

Though I continued to read for the rest of the week, we did begin chatting a little between stories. I had hoped that I would become his transcriber as he wrote aloud, perhaps suggesting a comma here and a fresher adjective there. However, there was no mention of his writing.

When I arrived on Monday of the third week, Anil was already finished with his tea.

"Let's start with a walk today," he said.

The going-out look wasn't that different from the staying-in look, except for one thing. The button-down cardigan was gone, replaced by a burnt-orange, cashmere V-neck sweater. It was as simple and beautiful a piece of clothing as I had seen on a man.

"Is Mira coming with us?" I asked. I was nervous about being out in the world with Anil by myself. I didn't know about his needs. I didn't know how much to dote on him when we walked down the street.

"She's not here. It's her time off when you come over. I've told her that I've survived sixty-two years without a full-time babysitter, but she insists. So it's just you and me."

I didn't immediately respond.

"You look disappointed," he said.

"No, no," I insisted. "I was just wondering about where we should walk."

I felt a letdown that had been building for weeks. I'd barely spent any time with Mira, but she had made an impression. Each morning, I arrived with the hope of seeing her. And each morning, I was disappointed. I wanted to believe that she was at home, quietly doing her own work in the other room. My throat and jaw had gotten accustomed to all the reading aloud, and I enjoyed the time I spent with Anil. But the real draw had been an imagined Mira behind the closed door. When I arrived, there was always a large, fresh pot waiting for us, enough for three cups of tea for Anil and myself. I'd assumed she made the tea and then went into her room.

As we stood there, getting ready to leave, I wondered whether I should end my days as the reader. The thrill of sitting next to Anil Trivedi had worn off after a couple of weeks, and these mornings were doing nothing to get my own words down on paper.

Anil grabbed his sunglasses from a side table near the door, a dark pair of tortoise-shell Wayfarers.

"Do you need a cane?" I asked.

"Do you?"

He walked out of the house without holding on to anything.

For the most part, Anil walked on his own, but every fifteen steps or so, he'd take my arm, find his balance, and then continue on as before.

"Is there someplace in particular you would like to go?"

"The campus isn't that far, is it?"

Anil walked with his head tilted slightly up so that he could feel the sun on his face.

"So tell me a little something about the neighborhood."

"It's a particularly good American dream," I said. "Wet."

There had been a bawdy dimension to some of our recent conversations. He'd wanted details about the women in my classes and the undergraduates walking around campus. Out of ten undergraduates you walk past, he asked, how many are transcendent or, as you say these days, *hot?* The higher the number, the better the campus. I was thrilled to have this conversation with an older Indian man. I didn't want to have it with my own father, and it felt a little taboo to have it with someone his age.

"How good?" Anil asked.

"The ranch-style houses are quite large, two, three thousand square feet. Most of the other houses are two and three storied with large front yards. Every fifteen or so houses, there is a new modern structure. Boxy, lots of straight lines, gray, with Japanese bamboo out front."

"Is that the new style?"

"For the younger, successful academics."

"I'd looked forward to more sun."

"There's plenty of it, but the sidewalks are filled with old, unruly oaks. The streets are nicely shaded by them."

We reached the one main road we had to cross to get into campus. The road was a loop that circled the university, and there was fast-moving traffic on it for much of the day. We stood on the curb and waited for the walk signal as cars barreled past us. Anil stood a little too close to the edge of the curb for my comfort. The passing cars were no more than two feet away from him. I wanted to place my hand on his shoulder and lead him back a couple of feet, but as I was about to, I stopped. I was assuming an intimacy between us that we didn't yet share. Talking about wet American dreams was one thing. I just stood there, hoping the light would turn green quickly.

"Nobody buys American cars anymore?" Anil asked.

"You can hear the difference?"

"There were a lot of Fords and Buicks when I was growing up in India."

Anil paused and listened.

"A Toyota, a Volvo, and a Mercedes."

I quickly looked to the right and saw the three cars as they drove away.

"It's a nice trick, isn't it?"

"How can you tell?"

"It was a hobby of mine as a child, and I've just stuck to it since. I get a little bored at the street corner, waiting for the light to turn. Of course it's a little more difficult in New York, where there are so many cars; but here there are fewer, and I have the time to listen to the particular hum of the engine."

Finally, the light turned, and we walked across the street, through another neighborhood, and on into campus. With Anil as a sort of literary ace in my pocket, I felt, for the moment, like I belonged among the oak groves, the rough-hewn sandstone buildings, and the long breezeways in the central quad that were always unseasonably cool. But I had not always felt this ease. When I first arrived on campus, I felt like I'd stepped into a massive, sprawling cathedral. I could look around, sit in the pews, marvel at the frescoes, and even attend a service now and again. But long-term worship? I would have to go elsewhere for that. I had been admitted to the university fair and square. And for this, I felt a deep sense of possibility. And yet I couldn't help but feel like I was some kind of imposter as I made my way to and from class.

As we walked, I told Anil about the Spanish architecture of the buildings, and as I said this, I realized I had nothing more to say about them. What made them Spanish? Certainly there were different periods and styles of Spanish architecture. Anil had asked what kind of trees shaded the street we had just walked through, and I only knew about the oaks. There were several other types I didn't recognize.

I suddenly felt panicked. What kind of writer was I if couldn't even describe to Anil what I saw around me? Wasn't an eye for detail a prerequisite? Had I been more curious, more interested, I would have known about the buildings and the flora. I'd walked around this campus hundreds of times since I had arrived but hadn't bothered to really look around.

After that first day of meeting Anil and Mira, I finally felt like I'd made the right decision in coming to graduate school. And since then, I'd been staying up late at night, ignoring the historiography of the British Empire, and reading the type of novels I wanted to write. But now I felt like I was just wasting my time here, tracing the outlines of a life I would never live.

"Let's have a little rest," Anil suggested.

I walked us over to a courtyard I liked. I'd wanted Anil to see a Rodin sculpture and only realized the foolishness of this right when we got there.

"So what are you reading these days?" Anil asked, as we sat down on a stone bench.

"You, of course."

I was a little embarrassed saying this, but I knew that a little flattery, even when he knew it was that, went a long way.

"And how is that going?"

"I'm enjoying it quite a bit."

I had enjoyed it to the extent that there was something unique about the experience of reading a writer and then spending large chunks of time with him. The writing was wonderful and polished and informative, but now it didn't do as much for me as it had when I first read him. Except for the first book and then the one on him and his women, the rest were a little too sentimental. There were one too many clownish, eccentric Indian uncles in the stories. One collected bowler hats, another read P. G. Wodehouse obsessively.

"I particularly liked *Blind Lust.*"

"I'm sure you did. You can imagine why it's my least favorite book."

"Well. You can imagine why it's my favorite."

I'd responded quickly for the sake of symmetry, but the second I'd said it, I regretted it.

"Let me say that again. It's a very sad book in many ways, and I like how you write about sadness. With such grace."

"Trust me. There is nothing graceful about sadness. So who else?"

"I was obsessed with the big boys in college. A lot of Hemingway. Perhaps too much. And then Fitzgerald and Faulkner. Carver. And now I'm reading all the Indians who're getting so much press."

It seemed that there was a new novel by an Indian writer coming out every week, earning extravagant praise in the press. These were the writers I liked, not only because they spoke to my experiences but also because they wrote in a new kind of language full of play, irony, and extravagance. And in all the reviews and the features about the cabal, Anil was seldom mentioned, and when he was, it was an obligatory paragraph so that the literary bibliography would be complete.

"Of course. The young bucks. They have no use for me."

This admission of being forgotten, said in a joking, dismissive manner, was masking a deep disappointment that after all these years of hard work, he was no longer read or, at the least, seen as a literary forefather. I couldn't be sure that this was how he felt, but there was something in his manner right then that suggested fatigue.

"They have plenty of use for you. Where do you think they learned their tricks?"

"Maybe I should hire you as my biographer."

"I mean it. You've shown them that big histories can be very small and personal. You haven't gotten enough credit for working through this years ago."

Anil thought about this for a second.

"I really appreciate you saying that," he said and gave me a light tap on my leg. "I'm assuming history essays aren't the only things you write."

"You'd be right," I said.

"So when do I get to hear some of your work?"

"I'm thinking never."

"That's the attitude that will get you right to the top."

"I have a few pieces that I wrote in college that I like, but I've done nothing worthwhile since."

"Why don't you bring something next time you come? I think I've had my fill of the *Economist* for now. I'd love to see what you're up to."

It made me nervous, but I really wanted to hear what he thought of my writing.

When we returned home, Mira was back and waiting in the living room.

It was the first time I'd seen her since that first day. She had not aged.

In the past few weeks, she'd occupied a prominent place in my imagination, in part because she seemed to be the opposite of my foray into dating fellow graduate students. Helen's ability to cut me off reflected her age and a deep cultural difference. Someone like Mira would never do something like that.

"Where have you been?" she asked, her voice raised. She'd been worried, and the relief of knowing Anil was fine was quickly fading and being replaced with anger.

"Sweetheart, we just went for a walk. Why are you home early?"

"I've asked you not to go out on your own until we've properly walked the streets."

"But I wasn't on my own. Rakesh was with me."

"How could I have known that? You needed to leave me some type of note."

"Rakesh is always here at this time of the morning. I assumed you'd remember."

Anil walked up to Mira to give her a hug. He was good at getting around, having developed a bat's sense of sound to get a feel for a place. He knew where the table was, and he could walk around it. Based on her voice, he knew how far to walk so that he could open his arms, move forward a few more inches, and hold her. But just as he walked up to her, Mira stepped back.

From where I stood, I could not see the expression on Anil's face. But I knew it had to be filled with embarrassment and anger. There was so much Anil could do on his own, but there were limits. And the unsaid rule between him and Mira was to not mention the limits and never ever to take advantage of them.

"I just don't like worrying like that," Mira said, realizing what she'd done. "I was so worried about you."

"Fine," Anil said, standing in the place where he'd been abandoned. "I'll leave a note from now on. I need to go to the bathroom now. Would you like a note for that?" He took a few steps and then stopped. "I'll be done in a few minutes. Maybe you can come wipe up for me."

"That's not fair," Mira said.

This phrase, more than anything that had been said or done that morning, set him off.

"You have nothing substantive to say about fairness. Please. You're welcome to write your Cheever shit on suburban angst, but please don't say one more word about what's fair and what isn't. Please."

"Anil. Can we do this after Rakesh leaves?"

"Why? I've never enjoyed privacy. Why start now?"

I was standing at the edge of the living room, Mira stood several feet away from me, and Anil was the furthest away, with his back to us. I wanted to leave, but things had progressed so quickly that I hadn't had the chance.

Without saying anything else, Anil walked out of the living room and into the bathroom.

"I'm sorry," I said to Mira. "I should have thought about leaving a note."

I wanted to take some of the heat off of Anil, but mainly I wanted to get into Mira's good graces. Seeing their domestic squabble felt a little like peeking into one of their diaries. I felt guilty but was still glad to know what I now knew about the cracks in their pairing.

"It's not your fault," Mira said. "He's such a stubborn man. He's had this insistence on doing things on his own forever. I just can't take the worrying anymore."

I could see her eyes filling up. She looked more beautiful than ever with the tears, and I wondered if Anil liked to make her worry to get back at the fact that he could never see what I was seeing now. He'd heard so much about Mira's beauty. And while he had her in every way possible, every man that passed by could have something that he could never have: the fleeting look of her, not the symbol of some woman in their past but the flesh-and-blood version of perfect beauty. He had to be angry about this.

"I'm so sorry," Mira said. "We barely know each other."

Her tears were like a siren. I moved forward and put my arms around her. In another circumstance, she might have backed off. But she seemed genuinely upset and out of sorts. She leaned into my chest and rested her head on my shoulder blade and tried muffling the sound of her crying. I could feel the wetness and the heft of her chest on mine.

A minute later, with Mira still in my arms, I raised my head out of her hair and noticed Anil standing there. He just stood there without saying a word. I let go of Mira.

"I should get going," I said.

When I returned the next morning, with a copy of my story in my backpack, Anil wasn't there. Mira was by herself in the living room. Ah, I thought. It was nice while it lasted. He's let me go.

"I called your home number, but I just got the machine," Mira said.

That message from Mira would stay there until the machine broke a few years later.

"Anil had to cancel this morning," she continued. "He forgot about a breakfast meeting he had with the director of the Center."

"I left early. And I haven't checked my messages."

I stood at the door for a few seconds. The only thing for me to do was to turn around and go back to my work at the library.

"Why don't you write down your mobile number so that you don't have to make an unnecessary trip next time."

I wrote my number on a slip of scrap paper, and I watched as she tucked it into her purse.

"So how do you like California living?" I asked. I didn't want to leave.

"These quiet streets are just what we needed. New York has been good to us, but we were looking for a break."

There was something there, but I was scared to ask. This was the first time Mira and I had really been alone together.

"Are you from New York?" I asked.

"The suburbs. Jersey. We came from India when I was ten."

"Really? I was eight when we came. What year?"

"Are you trying to figure out my age?" she asked, smiling.

I hadn't been, but it was something I had been wondering about. Anil was sixty-two, and Mira was his much younger wife. I'd assumed she was in her thirties or forties. At that point, any years above thirty blended into one another as one long descent into old age.

"No, no," I pleaded.

"1974," she said. "We arrived in 1974."

I did the math.

"Had you guessed younger or older?"

There was no right answer. Saying older was always a bad idea. And saying younger was just a failure at being charming.

"Twenty-six years between Anil and me. Do you find that too much?"

I did. Ten, fifteen years was one thing, but this difference placed her father issues up her sleeve and onto her forehead.

"No," I lied. "So how did you two meet?"

"The long version or the short one?"

"Long," I said, without hesitating.

"Good answer. People just ask about me because they have to. They want to know about Anil."

"Then give me the really long answer. From the beginning."

"Why don't you sit down for a moment then," Mira said.

She sat on the couch, and I sat on the adjacent chair.

"You don't need to sit so far," she said, looking straight into my eyes.

I moved closer. I could feel my teeth beginning to chatter.

"I grew up in a doctor's household. Both of my parents are doctors. Big house in suburban Jersey. I did a little writing in high school, but not much. Went to Princeton and studied econ because I liked it. My parents were happy with the decision. But they would have been genuinely happy if I'd done something else less, you know, Indian. After I graduated from college, I went to visit some family in Delhi. And I was talking to a friend of the family, and he said that they were looking to hire someone with a finance background. The Indian stock market was beginning to grow. And so I just stayed, and before I knew it, I'd been in Delhi for eight years. I loved it. But when I was getting closer to thirty, I was ready for a change. I had a good circle of friends, editors and writers and that type, and one of them suggested I think about an MFA. Business school was an option, but the idea of it sounded horrendous.

"So I applied to all the big writing programs and got in. Iowa, Columbia. I should have gone to Iowa, but the idea of going from Delhi to Iowa City was a little scary. I was already apprehensive about the move, and New York seemed a little better of a transition."

She didn't say so then, but later she would tell me that the main reason she was leaving Delhi was a dissolving marriage. The idea of divorce had not sat well with her Indian family there, and she was tired of their insistence that she give it another go. She had arrived in India, planning to stay for two weeks, had fallen in love with it and a man a few years older than she was, and stayed for eight years. She left heartbroken.

"I've always been out of step with age. In India, I was the youngest one in my group of friends. When I arrived at Columbia, I was one of the oldest. There were lots of kids who'd just gotten out of college. I spent very little time with them. Most of my friends I went to college with had settled in the city. I hung out with them in the evenings and wrote and went to my classes during the day.

"I met Anil in my second semester at Columbia. I was so sick of going to author readings. I hated them already, and there were so many that year. But I'd heard of Anil, and I went for the same reason everybody goes to see him. I wanted to see him perform his magic tricks. Of course he couldn't read from his book. But he'd memorized the first ten pages, word for word. I followed along for a while, and it was truly a remarkable thing. That may have been the first time that I fell in love with him. It seemed to me just so manly to take charge of his deficiencies like that."

The scene of a teenage Anil taking a bath flashed through my mind.

"And then he seduced me like he does his women. We spoke at the cocktail party after. He drank his scotch, and he conversed like normal. No mention of his blindness. He took interest in my work. Said that he would love to read it sometime. I spoke to him for an hour before the chair of my department came and took him away.

"The next day he got in touch with me through the department, and since then, we haven't spent a night apart. And for the most part it has all been good."

"So why did you need a break from New York?"

She had pointed to an opening, and I wanted to open. Badly.

She paused for a second. "What is it with you? You make it easy to talk and reveal secrets."

I shrugged my shoulders. It felt good to have a skill.

"It's such a cliché. He was having trouble writing. A lot of trouble. And to deal with it, he slept with a pretty female version of you. I knew it was coming, but I just let it happen. So here we are, taking a break from our New York life."

"He's a fool for cheating on you. He doesn't know a good thing when he sees it."

I have no idea how I said it without realizing what I'd said. Suddenly I got nervous that she would get mad at my slip of the tongue.

"No, he doesn't," she said and then laughed a little, finally registering what had come out of my mouth.

I followed her cue and smiled. She started laughing some more and then more, and then suddenly she was laughing out loud, from deep within her.

"I'm so sorry," I said. "I didn't mean to say that."

She got up and walked into the kitchen. She came back out with two glasses of water but left the laughter behind.

"I want you to know that I wasn't laughing at Anil," she said. "It's not even that funny or that bad of a slip. I've just needed an opportunity to laugh, to let go a little, especially after our little run-in yesterday."

"I'm so sorry," I said.

"No, no. I appreciate it. You made me feel much better."

She handed me the glass.

"In your morning sessions, have you two done any writing?" Mira asked.

"I've been waiting for him to suggest it. Just reading. I assumed he wrote with you in the afternoons."

Mira shook her head no.

"He's completed projects that he started before we met, but he's not completed anything new. I'm beginning to take it personally. If he doesn't start writing soon, I'm not sure what he'll do. If it's either me or the work, I'm not sure which he would choose. He's not happy with one without the other."

I felt like this was important information, but I didn't know how to interpret it or what to do with the knowledge.

"Are you a writer as well?" Mira asked.

"I'd like to be. I've written a few things here and there. I just can't imagine how Anil has written so many books."

"Little by little. He's got a lot of years on you. You'll get there."

It was my tendency to flee after a while from social encounters. I hated the idea of being perceived as someone who stuck around too long. But this time, I fought against my instinct to leave.

"I had read some of Anil's books before, but I had no idea that he was writing stuff like *Blind Lust*."

Mira smiled. "Are you reading that dirty little book?"

I felt chilly in the way I always did when sex was amorphously in the air.

"To be honest, I was riveted."

"I'm sure you were," she said, looking at me straight in the eye again, with a slight smile.

II. Winter Holidays

When my mother called the Sunday before Thanksgiving, I had not talked to her in six months, nor seen her in nearly two years. Even though I knew that my parents had made nice for years, I didn't think we were the type of family that could deal with actual estrangement or even have the capacity for it.

"I'm in San Francisco," she said, in the overly cheery voice she used when she wanted to avoid intimacy. "And Baba is here. Giving talks, meeting sponsors. I want you to see Him. He wants to meet you."

I could hear the capitalization on the phone, and it annoyed me.

My parents were divorced in everything but name. My father was on a yearlong contract in New York, living in a studio apartment his latest company had provided, helping them with their books. I'd been meaning to visit, but I kept picturing him alone in a small room at the end of a long day, eating bran cereal on his bed.

"I'm having a lunch this Wednesday at the apartment. Please come."

It was the apartment we'd lived in since elementary school, the apartment they still owned because the mortgage was so low, even though no one was living there. My father thought that if they kept the place, and didn't rent it out while he was away, he could somehow hold on to his marriage. I'd considered saving money and commuting down to school, but I'd wanted to get as far away from that place as possible.

I couldn't say no to her, and I couldn't face the lunch alone.

"I know this sounds a little premature, but would you mind coming with me to visit my mother?" I asked Mira.

Mira smiled a little mischievously. I explained my situation.

After that moment when Mira cried on my shoulder, I'd assumed that my reading days were over. But in the three weeks that had passed since, I'd been spending more and more time with Anil and Mira. At Anil's insistence.

We spent the mornings together as usual, and then I would go off to my classes. A couple of times a week, I would return in the evening for dinner. Sometimes, I left the house at night after Anil had changed into his pajamas. Alas, Mira always stayed a little more formal. Anil liked having me around. I wanted to think he saw me as a younger version of himself. We talked about books; he tried to convince me that baseball was more complex than cricket; I accompanied him and Mira to a few talks on campus. There was still no writing, just a lot of reading, now including works of history and politics placed alongside the magazines and newspapers that filled the coffee table. My story was sitting there as well, and I was waiting for Anil to bring it up so that I could read it to him.

At the same time, Anil set up moments when Mira and I would spend time together. He'd request that I go get something unnecessary from her, or he'd suggest she teach me the basics of Indian cooking. Over one long, unusually warm evening, she and I made samosas from scratch. My god, I've never loved flour, potatoes, and green peas more than I did that evening.

"My folks aren't living together anymore," I said. "And I'm not quite up to seeing my mother on my own. Maybe all three of us can go."

I really just wanted it to be us two, but that I couldn't suggest.

"Let me talk to Anil and figure out some logistics."

That Wednesday, the three of us got into my Taurus. It was an older model, which would have made me feel ashamed, but my father had kept it in perfect, meticulous shape. When I was growing up, it always annoyed me that he wouldn't let me eat in the car, but now I appreciated that particular bit of care.

Anil went straight for the backseat.

"Are you sure you don't want to sit up front?"

"He's quite sure," Mira said, smiling. She reached her hands into the backseat and tickled Anil's legs. "He grew up being chauffeured around. Why stop now?"

"I'm comfortable back here," Anil said. "You get used to it."

And so we were off, Mira and I in the front, Anil in the back, looking around as we drove toward the freeway. Anil seemed happy to be out and about. He'd been meaning to visit a cousin of his, the son of the uncle who'd originally brought him to America. We'd drop him off and come back when we were done with lunch.

After I'd been driving for ten minutes, it occurred to me that I had to be particularly careful on the road. I didn't want to be remembered as the guy driving the car when Anil Trivedi was killed in an instant by an oncoming semi.

"So Mira says your mother is a Sleep Baba devotee."

"Not a devotee," I responded, feeling a little defensive for my mother, even though she didn't deserve the defense. "She's interested in his ideas."

For two years, my mother had been living on an ashram in a remote village in South India. She first heard the Sleep Baba speak in San Francisco, and two weeks later, she packed her things, bought a round-trip ticket, and said she would be back soon. My father and I stood there, but we knew the part about coming back was a lie. My parents had not had a regular conversation in years, and I'd avoided being home when they were both there. A few kind words between long periods of silence was too much to bear. When she finally left, cool air returned to the apartment.

The Indian press had dubbed him the "Sleep Baba." Different spiritual men hawk different roads to enlightenment—hugging, sex, money, meditation. The Sleep Baba believed that humans experience far too much sensory stimulation, and the only way to counter it is to, as the Sleep Baba was often quoted as saying, *return to life as a child*. Sleep twelve hours a night, and take a two-hour nap in the remaining twelve hours. If he hadn't taken my mother away, I might have given him credit for giving the middle finger to the demands of capitalism.

And so yes, she was a devotee or, alternately, a cult member. But who wants to admit that about one's own mother?

"So what's the story with mom and dad?" Anil asked. "We don't hear much about them. Come to think of it, I'm not sure you've said anything."

"There's not much to say."

"There's always something to say," Anil said.

"Divorced but not divorced," I said, feeling a little sick to my stomach. "Your parents still alive, Anil?"

He shook his head no. "My father died early, soon after I published my first book. My mother several years later. I miss them, but I got freed from their presence relatively early in life."

I turned to Mira to hear about the state of her parents.

"Mira is being coy. But her parents have this perfect marriage. They met when they were eighteen, and I don't think they've ever spent one night apart."

Mira shrugged her shoulders. "They're lucky. I'm lucky."

The moment after Mira said this, she disappeared into a bit of privacy that lasted for the next several minutes. She looked out the window at the passing yellow hills.

"I hope you don't mind that I'm taking Mira with me," I said, finally breaking the silence. "I need a buffer."

"No problem. Mira is the perfect buffer."

We dropped Anil off in front of a large Victorian in Noe Valley. I waited in the car while Mira walked him to the front door, chatted a few minutes with Anil's cousin, and then returned.

"Gay as the day is long," Mira said as I drove away.

She looked excited.

"Is that news?"

"This is the first time I've met him. I don't think Anil has seen him for years. If nothing else, he'll kick-start something in Anil's writing. One more layer to his long-standing Trivedi family saga. He's always wondered why there wasn't someone gay in the family. Statistically it didn't make sense. He'll dictate some notes to me on the way home."

I drove across the city, toward my old neighborhood. I'd spent enough time with Mira to no longer feel the nerves. Now I was just reveling in my moments alone with her.

The closer we got, the foggier and colder it became. The studied hipness of the San Francisco we'd just driven through—the sleek bars nestled between old taquerias, minimal boutiques where the designer made dresses in the back room on an old Singer sewing machine, brunch spots where customers stood in line on a Wednesday morning—didn't stretch to my old neighborhood. Here in the outer Sunset, the bars opened early and closed late, and the patrons stayed for so long that they could only afford cheap beer. The streets were clean and orderly, but the façades of many of the houses had turned shabby. San Francisco's bit of East Berlin. Our apartment was on a corner, a narrow three-story place. We had the penthouse.

I buzzed up and then opened the building's main door. Just then, my mother opened the door upstairs.

"I forgot I still have a key," I yelled up.

The moment I stepped into the apartment, I suddenly felt embarrassed.

The apartment had a living room, a kitchen, two small bedrooms, and one bathroom. Six hundred square feet at most. My mother had opened up all the shades and the windows to get the air through. We used to keep the windows open, even when it was too cold, to make the apartment feel spacious. Heat could really shrink a place. There were nice *dhurries* on the ground, Mughal miniatures on the walls, and a couch and love seat set from JC Penney that had worn well over the years. But nothing could disguise the modesty of the place. What was I doing bringing Mira here with me? She'd described her New Jersey childhood and life in Delhi and New York, and it seemed very far away from a small, sunless apartment at the far, fogged-in end of San Francisco.

But I set the worry aside when I got a good look at my mother.

In the photographs of her as a young woman before her marriage, she wasn't beautiful but was pretty and well put together, her face long and thin. But in the years that had passed, the face had hardened. She seldom smiled in photographs, and her mouth had settled into a frown.

The woman standing in front of me wasn't just the woman from the early photographs but someone else entirely. She looked much younger. When I saw her last, there were streaks of prominent gray in her hair. They were gone. If she wasn't dyeing, there was money to be made in the sleep business. The Baba already knew this.

But more than the return to youth was the presence of joy. Her face had filled out a little, the frown lines had softened, and she stood there smiling, happy to see me.

"Hey, Ma," I said.

"*Cam beta?*" How goes it, sweet son?

She had always had this maddening skill to be, at one moment, distant and gone, but at another, the lilt in her voice, soft as a meadowlark, could contain such intimacy and care, enough to make me feel completely protected from the world. I wished this second version always appeared, but it was the first that I had gotten with greater frequency. Right then, despite everything, I was happy to see her. I'd missed her.

"This is Mira Trivedi. A friend. I work for her husband."

"Welcome, Mira." My mother was graceful as ever, and in that moment her face seemed to glow. Even in the dark periods, she always dressed well and maintained a good front with guests. Usually when she was socializing, she wore an expensive silk sari with strong, subdued colors. But today, she was wearing a quieter sari, off-white with a dark border and perfectly pressed. She had a bit of gold around her neck and the usual diamonds in her ears. She looked attractive.

"Baba," she said. "This is my son, Rakesh."

I'd expected the Sleep Baba to be a spiritual diva, with a huge entourage and a bloated self-confidence. But in that moment as we stood there, he seemed perfectly normal except for the flowing orange robe he was wearing. He was a trim, compact man in his early sixties who obviously took care of himself. Even though he was wearing loose clothing, I sensed from his lean face that he had sinewy, peasant muscle covering his body. Without the robe, he would have fit right in as a well-tanned, successful Hollywood producer, driving around Santa Monica in a late-model silver Boxter.

I'd imagined the lunch would be for five or six, but it was just the two of them. I was glad that Mira was with me.

"Come," the Baba said, tapping on the space next to him on the beige couch where he'd stayed seated since we entered. "Sit with me."

There were probably hundreds and thousands of people who would've killed to receive this invitation. I was just annoyed that he was sitting on my father's end of the couch.

I didn't want to admit it, but there was a warm energy in the apartment, not that different from the lively calm inside a church or temple.

"Your mother tells me you're doing a graduate degree in history. I'm happy to hear that."

It was the first time any of my parents' friends had been positive about the decision I had made.

"As the English like to ridiculously say, I read history at Oxford," the Baba said. He paused to consider what he was going to say next. "I used to teach a little. Sitesh Das is my birth name."

I looked straight at him. "Are you serious?"

He shook his head yes, a little meekly to not make a thing of it. But it was information he wanted to convey to me, perhaps as a way of making a connection. "It was a different life."

Sitesh Das had written his first book on the Mutiny of 1857 and swiftly turned everything that had previously been said on the topic on its head. At that point, he could have spent the rest of his life, with the book as his ace, going from university to university, getting paid extravagant sums so that he would be the star on a university's roster. But five years after that first book, he wrote a thin volume on peasant movements in nineteenth-century India that forced the remapping of most historical debates, not only within Indian history but within the discipline as a whole. Anyone wanting to say anything about pissed-off peasants had to first deal with his ideas. He was big before, but now he was supersonic. The Mick Jagger of the archival crowd, with a dash of J. D. Salinger thrown in. He wrote his two big books and then disappeared.

One afternoon, he left his book-filled office at Columbia, his lecture notes on Gandhi's autobiography for the following day on his desk, his wife and two children at home, and never returned. There were whisperings that he'd gone crazy and was quietly shipped to an asylum.

"I don't understand. Nobody recognizes you?"

"I'd like to think I've been reborn. I also lost quite a bit of weight."

"Why did you leave your job?"

"I'd reached my limit. There were other things for me to do. Luckily I'd been successful, and leaving didn't seem like that big of a thing."

I didn't know then to react to this sentence. But now I suspect it was a dig at my father.

"For well over a decade, I traveled, spent time with Buddhist monks in Japan and surfers in Java, and thought hard about what makes a good life. I couldn't get the adequate answer from writing my books and teaching undergraduates. Don't get me wrong. The academic life is a good one. It just wasn't for me."

While we were talking, my mother and Mira sat there and listened. In another circumstance, they would have started their own conversation, but my mother had become accustomed to listening when the Baba was talking. I quickly looked over at Mira, and she gave me a warm smile. While no meek woman, Mira had gotten accustomed to moments with Anil and his male friends when they did all the talking.

"So how's school?" my mother asked when there was a pause in the conversation. "Is it going well?"

"It's fine. It's much harder than college, but I really like it."

"What kind of classes are you taking?" Baba asked.

When I told him, he asked about the books I was reading. For a few minutes, we talked about them as he peppered me with questions. And then he backed away, as if he'd remembered that he'd convinced himself that the earlier life was worth abandoning.

"You should come teach a class," I said. "I'm sure they'd love to have you."

"I don't think they'd like what I have to say now."

I didn't like his presence in our apartment, but I liked the idea of being the one who'd brought Sitesh Das in from the cold.

"In addition to class," I said, turning to my mother, "I've been working for Mira's husband."

"What's your last name?" the Baba asked Mira.

"Trivedi."

"Your husband is Anil?"

Mira nodded her head yes.

"Tell him I say hello. We met years ago. We had a friendly disagreement about the British in India. He's a bigger fan than I am."

"I don't think he's a fan," Mira said. "He's just objective."

I knew that Sitesh Das would have sliced up the idea of objectivity. But the Sleep Baba just let it roll off his back.

My mother got up, went into the kitchen, and came back a minute later.

"Let's eat while the food is warm," she said. "Come Baba."

She'd prepared lunch. Every couple that has stayed together for a long time has one issue that encapsulates the growing rot. For my parents, it was food, and how my mother cooked far too richly, and that it was literally killing my father.

For lunch that day, she'd cooked a subtle, low-oil meal, heavy on vegetables, low on starch.

Over lunch, I'd expected the Baba to talk and the rest of us to listen on the virtues of getting plenty of sleep. But instead, we talked about issues—the conflict between India and Pakistan, his admiration of the Israeli army, the benefits of socialist China versus democratic India, Bill Clinton's love of women and the troubles that ensued.

"He needed to come see me, and I would have fixed him," the Baba said, smiling. He seemed confident that he could fix Clinton's libido and yet aware of the absurdity that sleep could cure a taste for lines of women.

I arrived prepared to not like the Sleep Baba. And when I saw that it was just he and my mother in the apartment, I refused to let my mind believe the worst. But slowly, I let down my guard. He had good conversational range, and all that sleep had done nothing to dull his self-awareness. "I know there's been many of us trying to make money off of magic cures. But this really works, or at the very least you feel rested, which is important. I've met Deepak Chopra. Maybe the guy is a good medical doctor, but he's an idiot otherwise."

For a few minutes, I stopped paying attention to the conversation and just sat and enjoyed my mother's cooking, savoring her signature lentils, with heavy doses of fresh lemon juice. It had been a while since I'd eaten her food. And it occurred to me right then that when she died, she'd take this taste, and the direct line to my childhood, along with her. This thought made me sad, and I decided that I was going to talk to her, work through whatever was between us. Perhaps with my father away, we could speak freely.

When I rejoined the conversation, we somehow were on the topic of children, and Mira was asking, "So what then do parents owe their children?"

"Absolutely nothing," the Sleep Baba responded. The omniscient tone that he'd kept in check before was now in full messiah effect. "Well, that's overstating it. We feed them, we give them shelter, and we do the necessary things that need to be done. Keep them out of harm's way. The one thing I agree with in American life is that children be cut off after a certain age. And the one thing I really disagree with in Asian life is this idea that children owe their parents gratitude for bringing them up. They owe them courtesy and goodwill but nothing beyond that. Western psychiatry likes to boil everything down to childhood and the relationship between parents and their children. It believes that parents mess their children up. They don't. Children mess themselves up. That's why I encourage childlike sleep. We need to return to our child selves but with the knowledge we have accrued as adults."

I didn't feel like getting into it with him, but he was entering sensitive territory. My mother owed it to me to be my mother, to continue being a wife to my father.

"Sitesh, you have children, correct?"

"I do."

"Well then, you'll have to allow that the parent-child relationship is a little more complicated than that."

"It is and it isn't," my mother said. "After a certain point, people have to take responsibility for themselves. Parents need to live their lives, children need to live theirs. And everyone needs to forgive a little."

I looked over at my mother. I expected the tip of her sharp nose to be glowing, in the way it did when she argued with my father, and to see the old version of her back. But she sat there serene, doing her best, most sincere imitation of the Buddha.

Despite the calm tone in her voice and her manner, I only heard reproach in those words. I couldn't understand why she was angry with me. I wasn't that demanding of a child. She'd said that I had needed to be constantly held for the first six months of my life. But I'd more than adequately made up for that initial bit of neediness.

"Maybe you're right," I said. "*Everyone* should take responsibility for the things they do." I stood up and excused myself.

This conversation was now headed into specifics, and I didn't want to have it in front of Mira and the Sleep Baba. It made me feel like a child, begging my mother for her attention.

I went down the hall to use the bathroom. I stayed in there for a minute longer than I needed. Though my mother's words were buzzing in my ear, I was actually feeling pretty good about standing up to the Baba's ideas and disagreeing. In my seminars in school, I made good, solid comments, but I never disagreed with anybody. Now that I'd disagreed with the master in my field, I felt I could go back in there, be courteous, and end the lunch on a relatively good note. Perhaps I needed to come to terms with the fact that I was not going to get what I wanted out of my mother, which was nothing more than to feel like I could look to her for emotional comfort.

I put a little water in my hair, pushed it back, and then walked out of the bathroom. But instead of going back into the living room, I turned left and went to take a look at my old room. Before I stepped in, I glanced into my parents' room across the hall. Next to the bed were two different suitcases, unzipped, with clothes falling out of them. The bed was made, but from the wrinkles in the bedspread, it was clear that it had been used the night before. I quickly went into my bedroom. It was untouched. I tasted a bit of bile at the back of my throat.

"Oh, Mira," I said, running into the living room. "We were supposed to pick up Anil half an hour ago."

I looked hard at Mira as I said this.

"Of course. Anil gets very cranky when I'm late."

Mira thanked my mother for the meal. I waved at the Baba from across the room and then said, "See you soon, Ma," as if I were just running down to the corner store for milk. I couldn't look at her.

And two minutes later, having said our quick, rushed goodbyes, we were walking down the stairs of the apartment building. I drove all the way down to Ocean Beach without saying anything and parked the car. We weren't due to pick up Anil for another hour.

We sat there for a few minutes, watching the choppy, unruly waves. There were a few surfers out, but they were mostly catching the whitewater. Without meaning to, I suddenly teared up. And by the time I realized I did, I couldn't hide the fact. Mira looked over and pulled my head onto her shoulder and gently scratched my head as I made my way through some overdue sobs.

"You all right?" Mira finally asked.

I didn't know what to say. When my mother first left, I had assumed that she was one among hundreds and thousands who had left their lives for what they thought was a better one. That stung, but I could manage. Up to the moment I entered the apartment, I had convinced myself that there was some uncrossed line between her and the Baba. And even when I saw it was just the two of them there, I kept my imagination in chaste check.

My mother a sexual being with needs fulfilled by a handsome, successful man who wasn't my father? It was far too much for me. I wanted to be mature, to have a contemporary, ironic sensibility about these things. "Oh yeah," I would say at cocktail parties, "my mother is sleeping with the Sleep Baba." But I had grown up in a household where the sexual lives of my parents, much less anyone else, was never a subject of conversation or even passing reference.

"You have to give her a chance to be happy," Mira said. "Besides the little you described, I don't know what she was like before. But today, she looked content. I know it hurts, but she probably wasn't getting happiness from your father."

"What's wrong with us?" I asked. "And what does she have against me?"

Mira knew not to say anything.

"So what set you off earlier?" she asked.

"An unmade bed."

"I can see why that might make you want to flee. I'm not sure how I would have reacted if that were my mother. I may have come back from the bathroom and insisted that they cease, desist, and never make mention of it again. I would have made them promise. At least you were mature enough to not make a scene."

She paused for a few seconds but then continued, this time no longer speaking as the daughter. "Rakesh, your mother is a beautiful woman. Perhaps more than you realize. It's probably something a son doesn't want to think about. And I'll guess that she has spent her whole life spurning the advances of men, denying a fact that has been made clear to her day after day. She may just want an opportunity to breathe, to be a little free."

As I listened to her, I continued to stare out at the ocean, and then I wiped away the salty taste of tears from around my lips. It's now hard to remember just how things progressed from there. Mira may have been trying to comfort me with a peck on the cheek. One moment I had been all tears and self-pity, and the next, Mira and I were kissing like a couple of high school kids, first fumbling to get comfortable and then settling in. It was a high school moment I had longed for but never really had. Me and the pretty girl parked within earshot of the ocean, the windows steaming up with every moment that passed.

For the first several minutes, we stayed chaste, sticking to the kissing. But then my hands got a little restless, and though I wasn't thinking about this consciously, I knew I had to treat it like a one-off event. And with that in mind, I moved my hands from her shoulders down to her breasts. I had been watching the heavy movement of them beneath her clothes for weeks, and I had pictured them in every which way.

But the second I touched one, and before I could really experience the pleasure that came with it, Mira quickly backed away.

"Oh no," she said. "What the hell am I doing?"

"Making me feel better?" I said.

She gave me this smile, and the second I saw it, I moved back toward her lips.

"We can't do this," she said, holding up her hands.

As much as I had liked the sensation of kissing her, for it was undoubtedly some of the best several minutes of my life, something about it also felt strange.

She got out of the car and began walking toward the beach. For me, it was the start of something I desperately desired, and it was helping me quickly forget my mother and the Sleep Baba. But for her, it seemed like we'd tipped off a chain reaction that frightened her. Did she have doubts about Anil? After seeing her parents' perfect marriage for years, had this bit of betrayal sullied her chance at that kind of happiness sometime in her life? For the next fifteen minutes, I sat in the car and then leaned against the hood while she took a walk in the sand, framed by the rough water and the gray sky.

For the first several minutes after we picked up Anil, we drove in silence.

"What's going on up there?" Anil asked. "Why so quiet?"

I looked over at Mira, but she insistently kept her eyes on the road. We had not made eye contact or talked since she had gotten back into the car. When I tried to say something, she just shook her head.

142

"The Sleep Baba wanted me to say hello to you," she said to Anil. "He said he met you years ago."

She told him the story of Sitesh Das.

"No kidding," Anil said, sounding nearly giddy in hearing this information.

The phrase—*no kidding*—was something I often heard my father use.

Anil and Mira got into a conversation, first about the Sleep Baba and from there about people and places I didn't know. It was as if Mira was trying to show me—or show herself—that there was a whole swath of life between her and Anil that I had no access to. She kept the conversation limited to the two of them and made no attempt to loop me in. By the time Anil reported on his time with his cousin, I just stayed away and listened. There had been times in the past when the distance between Anil and Mira seemed great, but right then she was being very attentive as they talked, and they were now hidden away in an intimacy that I couldn't pierce.

In a matter of an hour, I had gone from being in her arms to feeling like a chauffeur as we made our way home.

For years, I had been the boy in the backseat of the Taurus, my parents up front arguing in silence. I was still somehow in their orbit; they were responsible for me, I was responsible for being their son. But now, sitting in the driver's seat with the illusion that I had moved up from the back, my mother well behind in the rearview mirror, my father across the country, and Anil and Mira insulated together, I felt terribly alone. Later, these few hours would feel like a primer on the cruelties of adult life. But right then, the only thing that appealed to me was the thought of a long, deep sleep, a return to life as a child. Fucking Sleep Baba.

"Make sure to jot down some notes when we get home," Anil said to Mira.

For Anil, anything and everything was worthy of note taking, potential material to be used later, even if the experience was not his own.

For the rest of the drive, Anil talked about Sitesh's books. "An arrogant bastard but a sharp, expansive mind."

When we reached their house, Anil asked what I was doing for Thanksgiving. I suspected that Mira didn't want to spend it with me, but I was too blinded by the taste of her mouth to think clearly.

"No plans."

We spent it together, along with some other folks from the Center. I ended up sitting next to Anil, watching Mira across the table being charming to a couple of older men. For every five times I tried to make eye contact with her, she made contact once. I was developing my own Thanksgiving tradition: meals with unavailable women.

That Saturday, as scheduled, Mira and Anil left for New York to spend the month of December.

After they left, I kept myself busy for the next couple of weeks by writing final papers. But the moment I turned everything in, I felt restless. I couldn't imagine how I was going to spend the days until classes started again. I had no interest in doing any of the things I was supposed to do during my break—seeing friends, going to the movies, or driving up to the snow.

I missed seeing Anil, but what I really missed was Mira. I had fallen in love with her, first with the idea of her and then with the actual person during the lunch with my mother. I had never cried in front of a woman before. I felt like Mira understood some core part of me that seldom appeared in the light.

On a whim, I bought a ticket to New York. I kept telling myself that it was the right thing to do to spend Christmas with my father. But I was hoping that Mira and I would somehow have the opportunity to take a long walk through Central Park on a crisp, cold afternoon. That seemed like a good New York thing to do.

Two days before Christmas, I flew from San Francisco to New York. My father was at the gate at JFK to greet me. I'd told him that I'd find my way into the city, but he'd insisted. Except for the thinning hair on the back of his head, he was as bald as ever, and he'd shaved the mustache he'd worn for years. In another circumstance, it might have made him look younger, but now, set against a brightly lit airport terminal in the middle of winter, he looked stripped and bare.

"Rakesh. Welcome to New York."

My mother withheld; my father gave excessively.

He stepped in and gave me a hug. The intent was pure, but the execution was poor. We stumbled with the correct placement of our heads.

He handed me a small, canvas grocery bag that included a scarf, gloves, and a fleece hat.

"The temperature has dropped," he said, pleased. "We may have a white Christmas."

As we stood waiting for my bags to arrive, neither of us said anything. We'd always gotten along and understood each other, but we didn't have much to talk about. We weren't shy, but around each other, we slipped into an awkward silence.

"So how's work?"

I didn't want to ask, but it was the only thing that I could think of after nearly half the passengers had picked up their luggage.

"It's not perfect. But it's really not that bad."

He often exaggerated his cheer, but work was a topic that he spoke about with economy and honesty. He'd trained as an accountant, and I assumed that in the glories of litigious capitalism, there was always room for one more numbers man. He always found a job but was also one of the first to be let go when the cuts started. He was very competent, but his instinct to be friendly and kind to everyone had gotten in his way.

"They're saying they might have work for me through the coming year."

"Is that good news?"

"Very good. At this age, I don't want to get accustomed to yet another new city. But I like it here. You'll see. You might like it as well."

The finance job I'd declined after college had been in New York. My interview was the only other time I'd been here.

We got my bags, and I followed him outside. It was far colder than I'd expected. I stepped back into the terminal and put on the things he'd brought for me.

"We can take a bus or something."

My father waved this idea away.

Ten minutes later, we were in a cab, headed out of Queens, toward Manhattan. I'd been scared of how he'd get on in a decidedly unfriendly city like New York, but my father was displaying an unusual comfort and mastery over his new domain. He didn't look around as he walked; he knew his destination and went straight to it. In the cab, he leaned back and rested his right foot on his left knee and then commenced to play tour guide as we drove over bridges and saw buildings in the distance.

"Somewhere over there is the pretty lady," he said, pointing out the window to the left, toward Liberty Island.

For a second, I thought he was talking about the blonde in the cab next to ours.

A while later, the cab stopped in front of an Indian restaurant on the corner of Twenty-Second and Lexington. There were consecutive Indian restaurants up and down both sides of the street. We walked into one called the Vegetarian Palace. There were small, red Christmas lights in the window and on the walls inside. They were meant to create cheer, but they had nearly the opposite effect.

"*Mehtaji*," the owner said, as we walked in.

The man was wearing a brown suit—two sizes too big—and was deferential in the way that Indian restaurant owners could be.

"This is my son, Rakesh," my father said. "He's been flying for hours and needs a proper meal."

"Ah, the scholar."

The owner took my suitcase, and I followed my father to a table. A minute later, we were seated, with a twenty-four-ounce bottle of King Fisher between us.

"Once a day," my father said. "They say that hops are good for urinary health."

"Is that true?" I asked.

"I don't think so," he said, right before taking a large sip.

I was glad I'd made the trip.

The restaurant was half full and had that sadness that vegetarian restaurants—with their limited, peculiar clientele—have on a cold winter evening, a few days shy of a major holiday. My father waved to two different people eating their dinners on their own. The first was another Indian man around his age, and the other was a white woman in her early fifties, her hair the silvery shade of gray.

"Do you eat here often?"

"Four, five nights a week. He knows what I like, and I've done the math. It's cheaper for me to eat here than to buy all the ingredients and cook it myself. And you'll see. My kitchen is not fit for cooking. It's ideal for boiling small amounts of water."

The waiter came by with two *thalis* full of food.

"You have this every night?"

He shook his head. "Special occasions."

I could see why he ate here. The food was full of flavor but not saturated in oil. The chefs in the back took the time to cook. They served hot *sambar* in a small bowl, and the moment I was done, the waiter replaced it with a fresh one.

"The owner thinks steaming *sambar* is the key to a good meal. I've asked for a bigger helping, but he says that it will sit too long and get warm." He took a sip. "How's school?"

This was a difficult question to answer. The only real fight he and I had had was when I told him that I was not taking the job that paid me $75,000 and was going to graduate school instead, with an annual stipend of $18,000. I can now appreciate why he thought I was being a fool. In fact he had said exactly that: "You're being a fool. No one will offer you that kind of money again." He was right.

And so I couldn't answer the question honestly and tell him that I was bored with the whole thing.

"It's fine," I said. "You know I've been working for Anil Trivedi."

"*The* Anil Trivedi?"

My father was of that generation that admired Anil's perseverance and liked that he was such a great Indian ambassador to the
rest of the world. Like the Taj Mahal or fine Kashmiri rugs.

I explained that most of the job consisted of me reading articles
from newspapers and magazines.

"You're his eyes," my father said, thrilled at both the turn of
phrase and the fact that I was, actually, Anil's eyes.

"I guess. After I'm done reading, we discuss some of the stories.
He is really a remarkably sharp man. All that they say about the
blind is true. All his other senses work at a very high level. He senses
things, picks up what's in the air but not being said. Sometimes it's
a little scary being around him. He can sense what you're feeling."

We ate quietly, and after we were done, we walked out of the restaurant, took one step to the left, and went through another door.
He lived right above all that Indian cooking. Such apartments
were once called efficiencies, and his place was nothing less than
efficient. Two hundred square feet at the most.

"If you don't mind, we'll have to sleep on the same bed."

The room was very small, most of it occupied by the full-sized
bed. There was a minifridge in one corner and an electric kettle on
top of it. There was an attached bathroom and a small closet.

"I know it's not much, but the company seriously subsidizes the
rent. They own it and give it out to contractors. Anyway, I spend
most of my time at work and downstairs."

I could sense the look on my face, but I couldn't get rid of it. My
place was bigger, sunnier, and more alive. Is this what a lifetime of
kindness had netted him?

"It's perfect," I said.

I started unpacking my things but realized that I had nowhere
to put them.

While he was in the bathroom, I looked around the place and
then stood at the window looking out at the street below. Everything was shabby, from the chipped paint of the windowsill to the
overflowing garbage cans on the street below. My father had never
been a successful man, but now it felt like he had really fallen. He

was living alone in a tenement, and by comparison, I was living a princely life on a graduate-student salary.

He came out of the bathroom wearing what he'd worn to bed since I was a baby. A tank-top undershirt, white pajama bottoms, and a gold-embroidered *rudhraksha* necklace hanging down his chest. Time had passed. The flesh was soft, hanging below his arms and off his chest.

I quickly went into the bathroom.

When I came out, he was on his side of the bed, reading the paper. I laid down next to him. I wanted to say something, but I couldn't think of what exactly.

He broke the silence. "I'm glad you made the trip. There's so much I want to show you."

"I'm glad I did as well."

The next day, after a morning of looking at Egyptian mummies and the India holdings at the Met, we ended up in Chinatown for lunch. We settled in on the third floor of a four-floor dim sum place. Most of the customers were Chinese, but there were a few tables with young white couples and a few more with a single white guy in a table full of Chinese.

"So you like your job?" I asked.

"It's called *work*. If it wasn't, it would be play. But it's fine. As I said, there is a possibility of them extending it. After all these years, and all these jobs, I've realized that work is simply not in my stars. Well, I guess work and a stable marriage. I've tried so hard with these jobs. With each new one, I say that this one is going to work. But somehow, it just doesn't. I don't know what I'm doing right and wrong. Now, I just stick to the numbers and hope for the best. I've been waiting for the moment when my career will take off, and I'll feel that the work has been worth it. I am in my sixties, doing contract work. That moment is simply not going to come."

The polite response was to vehemently disagree.

He picked out several dishes from passing carts. "What do you hear from your mother?"

Since I'd run out of the apartment, I'd heard nothing from her. I assumed she was back in India.

"Very little," I said. "I saw her briefly in San Francisco about a month back, but that's it."

This little bit of information clearly hurt him. They'd been married for thirty years, but she didn't have the courtesy to call him when she was back in the country.

"I miss her. I can't tell you how much I wanted her to stay. But the fact is, she turned off years ago, and this is the only thing that has turned her back on. I desperately want her back, but if I had the choice between having her back the way she was versus letting her live the way she is, I think I prefer the latter."

I didn't know what was going on with my father. For years, my mother and I had complained about his inability to emote about the right things. He could emote but clumsily. And now it was coming out with clarity and precision. Either he was seeing a therapist, or someone was getting these emotions out of him.

We weren't eating lunch for that long, but by the time we stepped out, the sun had disappeared, replaced by gray clouds, and I could see the beginning of the snow.

"We have one more stop to make," my father said.

Through the light snow, we walked down to Wall Street. There wasn't the usual hustle, but there were still plenty of people around. The fresh snow put everyone in a good mood.

"This is the last of my speeches today. It wasn't good for me to pressure you to take that job. You had to make your own decision. And now, I'm so happy that you were strong enough to make it. I've never quite been strong enough. But I just want you to see this place. See the center of where the world's money is made. It may not last long here, but it will be here long enough for you to get your feet wet. In your lifetime, I think you'll go back to India, like we came here. That's where the money and the new life is. But I just wanted you to look around. I want you to *consider* the opportunities you have. They're remarkable."

As he asked, I did look around. I couldn't help but be taken by the mystery of the skyscrapers. Merrill and Lynch had walked around here somewhere.

"Thanks," I said to my father. "I really appreciate you showing me this."

He was treating me like an adult, and it was making me both happy and incredibly sad. There was something in the air about him, as if he were tying up loose ends.

The next day was Christmas. We'd never been a family big on holidays. Following my father's job leads, we had made stops in London and Toronto before ending up in San Francisco. In all that movement, my parents got tired of trying to fit into all the different customs and holidays they encountered. And so we went to our favorite Mexican restaurant for Thanksgiving, and we took a hike together on Christmas morning.

But waking up that morning, seeing my father still asleep next to me, I wished we had some set, more intricate ritual to follow. With a few more people.

That evening, there was a Christmas dinner at the Vegetarian Palace. When we got there, there was a large table for ten set up in the middle of the restaurant. My father introduced me to each of the other eight guests. They were all regulars at the restaurant— several Indian men, the rest white men and women, ranging in age from their midforties into their sixties. I sat next to Ruth, the woman I'd seen eating by herself that first night I arrived.

The waiters just started bringing food.

"Let me know if you need a little help navigating the dishes," Ruth said, winking.

"It's not exactly a Christmas roast," I said, taking a bite of a *dosa*.

"I've dealt with both Hanukkah and Christmas my whole life. I prefer nothing more than *idli-sambar* on Christmas night."

Ruth explained that she'd grown up an Orthodox Jew, then rebelled by marrying a Catholic, and then rebelled again by leaving him.

"Who are all these people?" I asked.

"Most of us met here. The chef is a quiet man but knows his way around the principles of hot and cold in a deep way. I haven't gotten sick since I started regularly eating his food."

151

For much of the evening, I chatted with Ruth about growing up Orthodox and why Indian meals were usually not served in courses. Every once in a while, she and my father made quick eye contact, but I didn't see them talk to each other all night.

My father was sitting at the other side of the table, talking to the two men sitting next to him. They kept ordering beers and laughing and eating. I'd not seen my father this happy in a very long time.

At one point, I looked to the table to the left of us, and the chef, the owner, and a couple of the waiters were sipping from hot bowls of *sambar* and eating these perfectly thin sheets of *dosa*. And beyond them, through the window overlooking the street, the heavy snow had finally arrived.

Even though I wasn't that tired, I went up to bed around ten p.m. I was having a nice enough time, and my father liked me being there, but I had the sense that I was cramping his style a bit. He'd accomplished what he needed to—he'd introduced his son to his friends. Now my presence was paying diminishing returns. When I said I was going up, he didn't argue.

I read from his stack of newspapers until midnight, and as I was falling asleep, I could hear the faint sound of the party in full effect. I didn't hear my father come in that night, and when I woke up in the morning, he was fast asleep. Usually a light sleeper, he didn't wake up as I showered and got dressed. I left him a note and walked out. The streets were empty, but when I stepped into a diner a couple of blocks away, the place was full and lively, mostly with older folks. I bought a *Times* and found a table.

I tried reading the paper but couldn't. Halfway through my eggs, I went to the cashier and asked if she had a phone book.

"I'm not listed," the cashier said and smiled. She looked eastern European. Her hair was pulled back in a bun, and she had on light makeup. In her clean, white shirt, she was well put together, which made her a hint prettier.

"I know where to find you," I said and paused, leaning my head forward and down toward her left breast. "Ania."

I took the phone book back to my table and looked through the *T*s. There he was, on East Seventy-Ninth. Calling at home was the less conspicuous option. "I'm visiting my father, and I thought that perhaps you were in town," I rehearsed. "I took a chance to see if you were listed. Funny thing. We walked right by your place yesterday on the way from the Met to the subway." The call at home would be a call to both of them. Not untoward at all.

I told myself I'd call after finishing the eggs, and then the bit of toast, and then the article on rising subway costs. And then it was just me, a check on the table and the phone book. If I was going to call, I had to do it while I was in the diner. I wanted to sound breezy, and the background chatter of the diners took me a long way there.

Anil picked up the phone.

"My dear boy," he said. The phrase was antiquated, and Anil's voice sounded different. "Why didn't you tell us you were going to be in New York?"

"It was a last-minute thing."

"When are you leaving?"

"Tomorrow morning."

"Well, come over for lunch today. There are plenty of leftovers from yesterday."

"Do you want to talk it over with Mira?"

"What's there to talk about? She'd love to see you."

"Can I bring my father along? He'd be thrilled to meet you."

"Absolutely," he said with an exaggerated enthusiasm.

Even though my father might have other plans, I knew he'd break them for this. When I got back to the apartment, my father was just waking up.

"Today?"

"Do you have plans?"

"Of course not."

For the next hour, he shaved, showered, and ironed his shirt and pants.

"They're informal," I said.

"This is not for them," my father replied, realizing that his thoughts were on public display. "This is my daily routine."

When we approached the prewar building, I felt a great bit of anticipation. This wasn't the stroll through the park, but it was a start. But the moment I stepped into the building and saw the marble floor and the gold details on the foyer walls, I felt embarrassed. Why had I invited Mira to our place in San Francisco?

We went up the elevator. Mira greeted us at the door and was moving forward as if to hug me but then seemed to remember that my father was standing right there. She gave me a look that I interpreted as forlorn. Was she annoyed that I had shown up like this?

"Your son is such a delight," she said, turning to my father. "So smart and so humble about it."

This compliment deflated me. It made me sound like a child.

The apartment was an airy classic six—a living room, a family room, a kitchen, and three bedrooms. My father's studio was roughly the size of the entryway. Mira led us into the living room, which was full of books, neatly arranged in one entire wall of built-in bookshelves. There was an enormous abstract on one wall—a cubist Krishna playing the flute—and a series of small canvases and photographs hung around it. Anil had bought the place years ago, and with the money from his books, the money his parents had left him, and the newly added wealth from Mira, the place was almost too nice to handle. I'd grown up thinking that couches were supposed to cost five hundred dollars and last a lifetime. I sensed that the clean lines and thick silk holding these couches together cost thousands of dollars and would be replaced after a few seasons. Anil, of all people, should have been a minimalist.

"Mr. Trivedi," my father said when we walked into the living room.

"Please call me Anil."

In his body language and in his overall tentativeness, my father had become the deferential Indian gentleman I so despised in the restaurant owner. It's fine, Dad. He's just a writer.

As we settled into our seats, Mira went and got water for us all. There was something different about her in this apartment. While she seemed more comfortable and lighter on her feet, there was also something weary in her manner. The cold weather had taken the color out of her cheeks.

She was not the only absent one. The lively Anil from the phone was gone. He was skinny already, but now he looked like he'd lost even more weight. And with a stubble that had gone unshaved for several days, his face looked hollow. It occurred to me that Mira might have told him about the kiss. Was this going to be an ambush, a shaming in front of my father? I began putting sentences together in my mind. "But Anil, it was almost as if you were pushing her my way."

I'd wanted my father to see how Anil fared so well despite being blind. But he was not putting on the show. As we made small talk, he stayed seated the whole time, as Mira ran around and did everything he asked. Tea, his sweater, the heater. Here was the feeble man I'd expected all along.

Back in California, there was a familiarity among the three of us. But here, things felt formal. Perhaps the presence of a father was making the mood more serious.

But it was over lunch—turkey, stuffing, mashed sweet potatoes, and a bit of holiday wine—that my father finally felt comfortable enough and started talking about Anil's book about his own parents. Through an intimate portrait of them, Anil had drawn an intimate portrait of a generation of Indians who were born around the turn of the twentieth century. These were my father's parents: high-caste Hindus, living well in the shadow of the British Empire.

"That's one of the great books. The great books of all time."

My father was nervous and so prone to hyperbole.

"Well, not all time," Anil joked. "Let's put it this way. Among Indian blind writers, I'm tops."

For a few minutes, Anil and my father traded stories about their respective parents. Anil was kind enough to listen as my father told stories about his family's political agitations against the British, and his father's time in prison with Gandhi. They were stories I'd heard countless times growing up. I took a sip of my wine, relieved that we'd gotten past the awkward silences from when we first arrived. Mira, however, was avoiding my attempts at eye contact.

The conversation about the book should have stopped there, but my father kept on with it, encouraged that he'd initiated a literary conversation.

"Your portraits of Motilal and Gandhiji, and then the young Nehru, are very well painted. You're a little quiet on Vallabbhai, but the Gujaratis have forgiven you. They were all such great men, and they had such good ideas for the country. The country's gone to rot now."

This was the way the book had been received and read for years. But when I read it recently, I realized that Anil was actually far more critical of this generation of leaders. When I'd asked him about it, he agreed. He said that he set out to be even more critical, but his editors had said that nobody would want to read a critique of that great generation. They want to hear the good things, not the things that made Gandhi human—occasionally randy and at times vindictive.

We'd had this conversation quite recently, and I could see Anil considering his options. He'd encountered yet another bad reader.

"You may want to go back to the book," he began friendly enough. But then his tone took a right into something hard and personal. "Read a little more *carefully*, take off the rose-colored glasses after all these years. I believe I'm far more critical. Gandhi was an egomaniac, and Nehru was the wealthy son of a reformed bootlicker."

My father's face remained unchanged, but I knew humiliation was lurking just below the surface. Anil was attacking: my father, the men he'd admired since he was a child, and his sense of Anil, whom he saw as an example of how to live gracefully in the face of catastrophe and setback.

I looked at Anil. And he looked right through me. I was sure he knew about the kiss. He was daring me to say something. But what could I say? Argue with him about the history, which I knew a little something about? Admit my love for his wife? I didn't contradict Anil, but perhaps more importantly, I didn't defend my father.

"I suppose we're all entitled to our interpretations of history," my father responded.

Mira knew that Anil wouldn't take well to this idea of history being a series of equal interpretations.

"Anil, can I serve you something else? Some more turkey?"

She only asked us after he'd waved her away.

"No," Anil said. "We are not entitled to our own interpretations. Some of us have done the necessary legwork to interpret the history correctly. What do you do for a living?"

"I'm an accountant."

"You don't see me coming into your office and telling you how to count your beans. Can't you extend the same courtesy to me?"

I'd never seen Anil like this. He was argumentative, but there was something more. He had the look of a poorly fed dog that had ended up in a corner and was now growling at anyone who approached. I wanted to say something, but I knew it would escalate things quickly.

For the remainder of lunch, Anil and Mira made no attempt to cultivate conversation. They made us feel like a nuisance, an unnecessary presence.

Finally, after all these months, I was angry at both of them, for their fragile, bloated egos, their self-importance, their luxurious days of reading and writing. They were a couple of fatted, spoiled kids living the good life I thought I wanted.

Barely an hour after we arrived, we left the apartment. Neither Anil nor Mira went through the motions of insisting we stay for coffee after I said that we needed to get going. Mira gave no indication for why they were behaving so poorly.

All the way back to his place, my father talked about how wonderful it was that I had introduced him to Anil. He was doing his best to hide the bit of hurt he felt.

"Everything I said on Wall Street still applies," he said. "But I have some better understanding of why you made the decision you made. It must be nice to spend time with writer types. I'm not clear how you're going to get there, but the life that Anil and his wife have is a pretty good one. They seemed to be in a bad mood today, but the overall life looks pretty good."

By the time we got home, it was past two p.m. I didn't have the strength to sightsee with him anymore, nor did I have the strength to sit and talk through the afternoon and evening. I needed a break, and so did he, judging from the speed with which he agreed that I should go check out MOMA by myself. By the time I got back, it was after five.

On my way back to the apartment from the subway, I slowed down as I passed the diner where I'd had breakfast that morning. Ania was still working the cash register, looking as neat and put together as she had been eight hours before.

"Are you here for the meatloaf?" she asked, pointing to the specials board behind her. "Or me?"

"Both."

"It's not very good."

"What?"

"The meatloaf."

"How about you? Are you good?"

I didn't usually flirt like this. But in the safety of a foreign city and my flight set to leave in twelve hours, I really had nothing to lose.

"I think so. But it's a question only you can answer."

"You should show me New York," I said.

"I get off in ten minutes."

"I need just a little more time than that."

"For what? To get permission from your parents to go out?"

"I'll pick you up in twenty minutes."

I'd have felt guilty about going out if my father had not stayed out as long as he had the night before.

I found him in the restaurant, having a *lassi* and doing some paperwork. I knew my father, and I knew when he was hurt. This time, he wasn't. Anil's words had stung, but he was concentrating on the positive parts of a new life he'd come to like.

"Are you hungry?" he asked when I walked in.

"I'm fine. I'm going to have dinner with an old friend."

"Fine, fine," he said. "I'll be here all night, and you have the spare key for the apartment."

I went upstairs and packed my suitcase and changed into a new shirt.

As I was walking toward the diner, my cell phone rang. It was Mira. As I stood there in the cold street, it took all my willpower to not answer. I didn't want to give her the out of a telephone apology. But I desperately wanted to hear her voice. I waited for a minute to see if she'd left a message. She hadn't.

I scrolled down the names on my phone as I waited a little longer, hoping that a message would still appear. I saw Helen's name in my list of contacts and, ignoring that voice that always thought through everything before acting, dialed.

"Hey, stranger," she said.

This was something in particular I really appreciated about Helen. She always picked up her phone.

We'd not talked since she left after our first year.

"Are you in New York?" I asked.

"I am," she said. "Are you?"

"You want to have a drink?"

"That'd be nice," she said.

A few minutes later, as I headed away from the diner and back toward the Upper East Side, I wondered about Helen's quick willingness to meet. Was she being kind out of guilt? I should have just headed to Brooklyn with Ania, for a nice evening that had neither a past nor a future.

I ended up in an apartment in the mid-Sixties, similar to Anil and Mira's, but this one was on the top floor. Helen greeted me at the door. She was wearing a black tank top, a simple, long cashmere sweater, and a pair of faded jeans. I remembered that I'd fallen in love with her elegant simplicity.

She stepped forward and without saying anything embraced me. I wrapped my arms around her, and as if by instinct, my right hand came to rest on her soft lower back. Her skin felt warm.

"It's nice to see you," she whispered.

She closed the door behind me.

"So this is Troy," I said, looking out into the living room.

"I guess," she said, sheepishly.

Down two steps from the entryway, the living room was large and airy with high ceilings. Where my living room at home had one sitting area, this one had three—one formal, one less so next to a fireplace, and yet another set among bookshelves filled with hardcovers and large art books. On one wall, there was a painting that couldn't possibly have been an original Klimt but very well might have been. The couches here made Anil and Mira's look plain. The far end of the room led to a terrace that overlooked Central Park and the glittering lights of the city beyond it. I was overwhelmed by the niceness of it all.

Helen had been very vague about the details of her New York life. She'd told me that she was an only child and that her parents were always out. We'd bonded over this. And while I'd been left alone in a tiny apartment, she'd been given keys to a much-larger kingdom. I'd seen my scholarship and everything that came with it as an arrival into a new, dazzling place. I realized now that for Helen, it had been a step down, a gap year visiting the Third World before she got on with the real business of her life.

"Shabby view," I said, stepping out onto the terrace. I walked to the ledge, looked over, but then quickly stepped back. I've never been suicidal, but I've always been scared to stand on a balcony or walk over a freeway overpass. I fear that my unconscious would override the rest of me.

"You never get used to it. In winter, it's particularly beautiful."

We went back inside and sat down among the books, and Helen pulled a cork from a new bottle of wine. I had always been impressed with her proficiency with corkscrews.

The wine and departmental gossip eased the initial awkwardness of our reunion. I told her about Sitesh Das.

"I don't understand. He just reemerged as this holy man?"

"We didn't get into it, but I don't think he's seen his wife and kids since he bailed. Now he lives on this ashram, and American CEOs pay thousands of dollars to come detox with him. He's a scam artist."

"And what's your mom doing with him?"

"I don't want to know. I'll be fine if I don't see her for a good long while. I realized this time around what I've always felt. She never wanted children. Or even to get married, at least to my father. But in India in the seventies, there was no agreed-upon language for that refusal like there was here. When I saw her, she seemed quite happy. And it was in direct relation to not being around my father or me. There's nothing I can do about that."

We drank that first glass quickly. We didn't need to be drunk to be around each other, but we had been good, happy drinkers together. The wine was easing both our nerves.

"Let me get something to coat our stomachs."

"Don't bother with anything. I just barged in on you."

I wanted to stay. I wanted to keep talking to her.

Ignoring me, she went and got an abundant platter of cheeses, crackers, figs, jams, dates, and thick slices of salami.

"Was this spread just sitting there?"

"My parents had a lot of people over for Christmas. There are plenty of leftovers. I was hoping for a quiet evening with just the three of us, but my mother thinks a dinner party for fifteen is intimate."

I'd not eaten since lunch, and then not very much, and so I attacked the cheeses and the salami.

"So what's up, Rakesh? I'm so happy to see you, but this is a little out of the blue. What are you doing in New York?"

I started by telling her that I'd come to visit my father.

"And was that a little better than with your mom?"

"It's been great. He's doing really well. He didn't come out and say it, but I think he's seeing this woman. Ruth. I've always hated that name, but she seems really nice. They were eyeing each other across the table last night over dinner. I wish he'd just told me what was going on with them, but he prefers it this way. I think I'm now officially American. Both my parents are seeing other people."

"And you?" Helen blurted out.

A part of me still thought she and I could be together, and seeing her had confirmed that. And that part almost stopped me from telling her about Mira. But she was also the only person I could talk to about this, the only person who might appreciate the contours of the situation.

"Wow. You're getting big-time. AWOL scholars and sleeping with the wives of famous writers."

I didn't say I hadn't slept with her.

"So what's going on?"

"I don't know. She's at least ten years older than I am. Why would she be interested in some no-name guy? But then she's the one who's flirted since we met, the one who kissed me first."

"You're a handsome guy. You're the first person I noticed at that start-of-the-year department party."

"Really?"

I liked hearing this. Despite the attention I had gotten from women over the years, I had never seen myself as being particularly good-looking.

"With Mira," I continued, "I'm not sure what I feel. I certainly don't want to hurt Anil. I really like spending time with him." I didn't want to openly admit that I also saw Anil as someone who could help me with my writing career. "But I feel crazy when I don't see her. I barely know this woman. And that was clear this afternoon. I wanted my dad to meet Anil, but they treated us like absolute shit. I thought we all had some connection."

Helen took a big sip of her wine and then another.

I suddenly felt like I'd said too much too quickly, and to compensate, I turned to Helen. "Sorry. Enough about me. What about this boy you left me for?"

"No, no. We haven't finished with you yet."

"My cards are on the table. I've placed myself in a ridiculous situation. I'm good at that, remember?"

In the one class we had taken together, Helen followed a similar pattern week after week. She would listen to the arguments and disagreements about the book we were discussing, and then after she'd heard what everyone had to say, she'd make simple, declarative statements that somehow cleared everything up and got to the truth of things.

"It seems to me that you have to wait this out," Helen said. "Be patient. They're married, after all."

"Yes they are, but Anil has been no saint in that relationship."

"Maybe that's why you should be."

This request for sainthood had far too many layers to peel back at that moment.

I could see that Helen was about to say something more but had pulled the sentence back into her throat at the last second.

"What?" I asked.

"You seem to be making a habit of being the other man," Helen said.

I could feel my entire back suddenly heating up. It wasn't a false statement, nor was it easy to hear.

"That's not fair," I said. "Before we got together, you never told me you were seeing someone else."

"I'm no saint in any of this. But I'm just learning to be a little more careful about people."

"I've been careful," I insisted.

"I'm sure you have."

I should have been angry and defensive with Helen. But I'd never known her to be malicious or biting for the sake of it.

"Whether it's a habit or not, I think I'm done being the other man," I said. "So what did happen with your Yale boy?"

"There's not much to say," Helen said, now looking past me. "I came back here to make things work with him, but he'd moved on. He'd been seeing someone else while you and I were dating."

"Why didn't you just come back to school?"

Helen shrugged her shoulders. "I don't know. We'd been together for a while. I was in shock. I've been pretty much sitting in this living room since I got back last June."

It was my turn for the successive, big sips of wine. Here we were, both heartbroken by different people.

My chest was in a state of frenzy. I was thinking about Mira, and then Helen, and feeling sick that Helen was dealing with heartbreak at the dirty hands of another man. I wanted us to strip down and get warm under one of those perfect down comforters she always had on her bed. But I also wanted to fly off that terrace and be very far away.

"Thanks for letting me come over," I said abruptly.

"Just sit for a minute, Rakesh," Helen said, placing her hand on top of mine. "Let's finish this bottle. I think this is the conversation we should have had way back when. I was just too nervous to have it. I shouldn't have disappeared like that."

"It was a little sudden. For a while we were spending so much time together. And then nothing."

"I know. I'm sorry. He was my first serious boyfriend, and I just couldn't face the fact that once we graduated from college, it naturally ended. I know everyone says this in situations like this, but it wasn't you. You were perfect. *You are.* You were the best part of my time in California. And then after I stormed off, I was just too embarrassed to come back."

"I wish we'd just talked," I said.

For the next fifteen minutes, we just sat there. Helen hadn't removed her hand from mine.

"I should go," I finally said.

"When will I see you again?" she asked.

I didn't know how to answer that question.

"Soon, I hope," I said.

Before going back to my father's apartment, I walked to Anil and Mira's building, hoping somehow that Mira would be out for a late-night stroll. I walked up and down their block several times but gave up after a few of the doormen along the street started looking at me with suspicion.

III. Spring Baseball

The winter quarter started. I attended new classes with the same sense of hope that I always had at the beginning of something new. Trying to keep Mira and Helen out of my mind, I went on two dates with a woman who'd graduated from my high school the year before me. I'd bumped into her at a coffee shop near my apartment. January passed. And then February.

I should have been the one angry and distant over how the lunch in New York had ended, but it was Anil who didn't call. As I was walking out the door that afternoon, he'd said that he'd be in touch once he and Mira got back to California. But I'd heard nothing from either of them. I assumed that they'd decided to stay in New York for a bit longer.

Finally, in mid-March, I got a call from Anil. On the phone, he sounded as if we'd talked the previous day. He made no mention of his silence.

"Can you come by tomorrow morning?"

Absolutely not. Not after how you treated us in New York.

"I want to talk to you about a couple of things, including your wonderful story."

"How's 8:30?" I asked.

When I arrived the next morning, the magazines and newspapers that usually sat on the coffee table were gone. In their place, there was a neat stack of three hundred manuscript pages and, next to it, my twenty-page story about a young man's bungled suicide attempt.

Anil looked no better or worse than when I had seen him last. I sat down on the couch, and Anil poured me our customary cup of tea.

"I'm sorry we've been out of touch. We stayed in New York a little longer than expected. I was being productive, and I didn't want to mess with things. But before we get to all that, let's talk about you. Mira read me your story, and then I had her read it to me again."

The idea of the two sitting around reading my story aloud, even before he told me what he thought, made all the time I'd spent with him reading, and the humiliations of the lunch, worth it.

"I really like Gautam Das," Anil began. "Naming a young man in crisis 'Gautam' may be a little heavy-handed, but I'll leave that up to you. But I believe in his crisis, even though he's living this very comfortable, bourgeois existence. Then again, who am I to judge that life? You get to him well. I've been thinking about him quite a bit for the past couple of days. I miss him. His pleas for help from parents who are unable to listen. That was heartbreaking. Character. That's what you're good at. You have a good eye for people's emotional tremors. If you weren't a writer, I think you'd make a great therapist. You can put character in your back pocket and move on to other things. And you'll learn those other things if you keep writing. My main suggestion is that as a writer you shouldn't be afraid to emote. Allow yourself the emotion you see in your characters. Be a little sentimental. I know you young kids frown on that. You want this smart voice that sees and understands all, with a tongue firmly planted in the cheek. But understanding is nearly impossible. Emotion is the thing that matters. It's the only thing that matters. You've got to be honest with yourself. And to your readers."

Anil placed his finger on top of the story and pushed it back toward me.

"I have one other thing I want to talk to you about."

Even then, I sensed that Anil had waited to read the story for as long as he had in order to get something out of me. I knew that, but it still felt so good to hear the praise. I desperately wanted to believe what he'd said. And what he'd said, though brief and almost a little simple, has stayed with me for years.

"Mira might have told you about some of our recent problems. I've been working on this book for a while. I've had a lot of starts and stops. But I'm just coming off of a good bit of work. I need a little help from you."

"What can I do?"

"First, I want you to read this whole manuscript. Once you know it, we will go through it paragraph by paragraph and get it cleaned up. I need to finish this before we leave in June. I'm giving myself a hard deadline. I know you have your own work to do, but I need your complete devotion to this. I was going to help you anyway, but if you can help me get through this, I will be your greatest advocate. Rakesh, I need to get through this, and you're the only one who can help.

"Mira has caused a work stoppage. I've been looking for her my whole life. The idea of her has driven my writing since I was in my early twenties. But now that I've found her, I can't do my work anymore. You've been around us. Sometimes it's good; mostly it hasn't been. This is my last effort. When I get this book done, I'll be done. And then it will just be Mira and I, and we can concentrate on her writing."

"Why me?" I asked, fishing.

"I like you. I like how you think. And now I like your writing. I have a good feeling that this is going to turn out well. I need you to infuse the book with your enthusiasm."

I was very happy to hear all this. But something in Anil's look and manner made me sad. His age suddenly felt palpable. He knew that his days were numbered. All of us know this, but he knew it more intimately and less abstractly. His body was giving out; his mental strength was not what it had been. I imagined the stakes for this last book, despite all his past successes, were now high and real.

I placed the manuscript in my satchel.

"It's the only copy I have."

"What do you mean?"

I'd grown up with computers, and the concept of backing up and then backing up again and then, just in case, emailing the document was second nature. A single copy seemed as antiquated as, well, a typewriter.

"Maybe I should just plan to read it here."

"Take it," Anil said, sounding a little annoyed. "But just be careful. And be back here in a couple of days."

As I walked out to my bike, Mira came out after me and closed the door behind her. She looked tired, as if she'd not slept in a month. She needed some time at Sleep Baba's ashram.

"How are you?"

She shook her head. She stepped up to me, gave me a hug, and then lightly kissed my lips. As much as I loved the feel of her, I felt guilty for betraying Anil at that particular moment after he'd just revealed a bit of vulnerability.

"It's been rough," she said. "He's unraveling. I don't know what's happened. When we arrived in New York in December, he suddenly grew depressed and moody. He kept asking for help with things he'd done on his own for years. Putting on his clothes, going to the bathroom. And then for a couple of months, he went on this frenzy of work, saying he was finishing something he'd started already. Fourteen-hour days. When he finished a draft, he decided we should fly back. We got back a few days ago. I'm so sorry about the lunch. We both acted shamefully. I was just glad to be needed by him, but I realize now that he was just pulling us both down into the muck."

"I was beginning to wonder if you two would ever call."

"We've been meaning to. But I think you'll be glad we didn't. It's not been pretty. Then he got it into his head as we were flying here that you'd be able to help him with his book."

"I don't think there's anything I can do that you haven't done already."

"I haven't read it. He won't let me. He used an old assistant with the transcribing."

I'd been looking forward to the reading, but it was starting to feel like too much pressure.

"You're making me nervous."

"Don't be. Just be honest. That's all he wants."

I made a move toward my bike.

"By the way," Mira said, touching my arm, "I really liked your story. I'm not exactly sure why Gautam wants to commit suicide. The parents aren't all that bad. But the story had such a pitch-perfect combination of humor and loss. I was envious of you when Anil asked me to read it again. And I'm envious of the story."

"I really appreciate you saying that." I wanted to ask more about the story, but there was something else more pressing. "Why did you just kiss me with him right inside?"

"I don't know, Rakesh. I really don't."

I leaned forward and kissed her back. The presence of her lips canceled out the guilt I felt about Anil and the anger I had toward Mira. "I'll see you in a couple of days. I've missed you."

Nervous and excited, I quickly rode away.

I went straight home and placed the manuscript on my desk. This was the moment I'd been looking for from graduate school: live work in front of me, not the death of archives. I started reading quickly, as if the pages held some answers to the complicated questions surrounding me.

In the first couple of pages, Anil explained that at this later stage in his life, he was returning to the autobiography that had started his career. He realized that he'd been given a chance to publish so young because of the novelty of what he was doing. For the few books that followed, he'd written about his life. But out of fear of being a narcissist, he'd turned away from himself. Now, he was coming home, back to his own story. He was going to re-recollect the first twenty years he'd worked through in the first book, but this time from the point of view of an older man who had smelled, heard, and tasted so much more. He said he hadn't read that first book for nearly forty years and that he had no intention of doing so now. The idea of this sounded promising.

The reading, however, turned out not to be much of a joy. There were plenty of rough pages, but the ideas behind the incomplete sentences weren't all that evocative. By itself, the material was interesting. But it was too familiar. Anil had thought that he would bring wiser, older eyes to the material, but it read like bits and pieces of things he'd written already. A greatest hits album. The book, and perhaps his life, was tired; there were no new insights left. Anil had run out. In his books, he was not particularly adventurous, but what he'd done was taken a close look at his life, his family, and his nation and found plenty of things to write about. He came back to the same people and places over and over again, but with each new book, he filled in the details about a person that had previously remained hazy, unexplained. But at this later stage, he'd filled in all the details, and no new people were coming and going from his landscape. The gay cousin had not made much of an impact.

I thought all this, but there was no way I was going to say it. It was not the type of thing that a young writer, the winner of an inconsequential undergraduate writing prize worth a hundred dollars, was going to say to a writer with books in the double digits. But I also knew that I needed to take a chance and say something substantive. He'd sniff out false praise. I rehearsed in my mind what I'd say, and I wondered what might happen to his relationship with Mira if this book didn't work out. I figured he'd appreciate my thoughts and then send the book to his editor for some real advice.

I finished the book by the following evening, but I didn't get back in touch with him for several days. I needed to get my thoughts together, and I wanted the appearance of having spread the reading out.

When I talked to Anil, I'd expected some form of rage or argument. Instead, he just sat there, as if he was hearing what he already sensed but couldn't quite admit.

"Have I run out of things?"

"Absolutely not," I said. "Maybe you're just not looking in the right places."

I had read all of his books and, at a gut level, felt like there was something missing, not only from this new book but also from everything else he'd ever written. I just couldn't put my finger on it.

"If you want me to write one of these American books about how I was fucked over by my parents, that's not me."

"You weren't fucked over by your parents, or you don't want to write about it?"

"Everyone is fucked over by their parents. That story isn't that interesting to me."

"What is interesting?"

"I don't know anymore."

"This is just my opinion. There is a whole generation of readers who don't know your work. Maybe this will introduce you to them. I just think I'm too close to everything you've written to be a fair judge."

"For an introduction, they can just go back to my earlier work. I thought I was doing something new."

We sat quietly for an awkward moment.

"Don't worry. I'm still going to help you. It took some courage to be as honest as you were." Anil paused and then continued. "You'll do well in whatever you end up doing. I wish I was more like you when I was your age."

"Anil. You'd published a best-selling book by the time you were my age."

"That's true," Anil said, needing to be reminded.

I stood up to go. "I should have asked you first, but I bought us a couple of tickets to see the Giants on opening day. Would you be interested in that?"

I'd bought the tickets because we'd talked often about baseball, and I knew how much he liked it. And I also wanted to spend time with him away from the reading. I'd never been to a baseball game, and going through this rite of passage with a blind man leading me through the logic of strikes and foul balls seemed perfect.

"It's supposed to be a beautiful ballpark," Anil said. "And Bonds in his prime? Of course I'd be interested in that."

A couple of weeks later, we drove up to the game. It was one of those sunny, cool days that San Francisco seems to spill out with embarrassing regularity. Anil looked chic in his Wayfarers and his cashmere Dunhill scarf as we walked to the stadium from the car. For a blind guy, he paid an awful lot of attention to how he looked.

"It's pretty stunning," I said, as I got my first look. "Beautiful red brick."

And it got even better as we found our seats along the third-base line, ten rows up. With a blue sky overhead and the sparkle of the water, it felt like we were on a flotilla in the middle of the San Francisco Bay. Opening Day at Pac Bell Park was perfect for a person like me who had minimal interest in the sport. And the Giants were a perfect team for me to follow. They had history, of course, but liking them was not predicated on knowing everything about their lineup in 1964.

"Did you spend a quarter's stipend on these?" Anil asked as we settled in.

"I actually used some of the money I've been earning from you," I replied. "So technically you bought these."

Anil never ate much, but soon after we sat down, he handed me a fifty and asked me to buy everything that came by: hot dogs, peanuts, chocolate malts, beer. We ate hot dogs and washed them down with beer, all before the first pitch was thrown. As he went over the rules with me again, I cracked open peanuts and handed them to Anil, while ordering a spicy tuna roll from a waiter who came around.

The opening pitch was thrown, and then the Padres came to bat. For the first inning, Anil concentrated on what was happening on the field. And for a few minutes, I closed my eyes along with him. The sounds suddenly became extremely loud. The people chattering close to us, the announcer calling up batters, the crack of the bat, the ball thumping into the catcher's thick mitt, a hot dog vendor, the beer man, and then of course the crowd, just happy that it was sunny, with a little breeze, and that there was glorious baseball being played in front of them.

At one point early on, the stadium went into a particular frenzy.

"Is he up?"

I looked toward the plate. Bonds was standing just away from it, swinging his bat around as if it was designed for more than just hitting a ball.

The first pitch came right over the plate, and he took a massive swing. Nothing. And then he watched three balls. When he walked to first base, the crowd went back to its subdued excitement.

For the early innings, we just sat, listened, and drank beer. I was discovering the joy of watching live baseball, which in essence meant sitting around, chatting on occasion, and waiting in anticipation for something big to happen.

Somewhere around the fourth inning, Anil said to me without taking his eyes off the field, "I think she wants to leave."

I knew he was talking about Mira.

"Who?"

"She's the only woman I've truly loved who's loved me back," he continued without bothering to answer my question. "But if she leaves, at least there'll be something to write about. God knows I've run out of things. You made this very clear."

"Did I?"

"You did."

"Has she said she's leaving?"

She'd not talked about it to me.

"No. But I can sense it. She's getting impatient with my needs. And she married a writer. I'm not doing that anymore."

"She married you, Anil. I don't think she cares whether you're writing or not."

"I care."

"That's fine. But she doesn't. And so you have nothing to worry about."

"It would be better if she left. What is she doing with an old man like me? She needs someone young, with his life ahead of him."

"You're not an old man. And she isn't your child bride."

In the fifth inning, another buzz passed through the crowd.

Bonds took a big swing at the first pitch he saw, before the pitcher thought too closely about walking him again. It quickly cleared the right-field fence.

Even I'd heard the loud crack of the bat, like a piece of wood that had just been hacked clearly in half. It was loud and quiet all at the same time.

"He's quite the hitter," Anil said. "Now he just needs to learn to start trotting around the bases a little faster."

By the top of the eighth, the seats around us began to empty out. We had some breathing room.

"Do you know how I became blind?"

I wasn't clear about the exact details. Everything he wrote was built on that original moment of trauma, but he had never presented it as trauma, just mere fact. There was some suggestion from his family that it was a question of fate, but as the recipient of the cruel joke by the gods, Anil was less receptive to the idea.

"Was it rubella?"

"Something like that. I wrote that it was something I had at birth. I grew up believing that I'd gone blind at the age of six months. Writing books is a funny business. You codify a set of memories. And people read your work, and now they have the same memories you have. You begin to feel like a spy, maintaining all these different identities.

"But the truth is I didn't go blind until I was two years old. At the time, we were living in the countryside. My father worked for the Indian Civil Service, and he was doing his time in the sticks, collecting revenue. We had a well-appointed government bungalow. It was a comfortable life. I was the firstborn. My parents were thrilled because things on the outside looked very good. They were aware that surface wasn't everything, but they also knew its importance.

"I was a fussy child. I didn't sleep well. I got colds often. One time, I'd been screaming for much of the night and through the morning. That day, my father needed to travel into a rural area, and he left early in the morning and would be back late in the day. He didn't want to go, but he also didn't want to stay home and hear me cry all day. At some point in the day, my mother just got exhausted and let me cry. She wasn't neglecting me. But she had had two years of me crying and had learned to take naps through my tears. It's a strong woman who can sleep through the wails of a toddler.

"My father returned that night, exhausted and hungry. The next morning, he thought about taking me to the hospital, which was a local train ride away. But he had some work he needed to finish. It was pressing, but it wasn't crucial. If he decided to take me to the doctor, the whole day would be gone. We'd taken the trip to the doctor many times before, and usually we returned with assurances that I'd be better by the time I turned two. They didn't call it colic then. They said I was one of those babies who was slower in building a curtain between myself and the world. The world, according to the doctor, overwhelmed me.

"Anyway, he decided to finish his work. And by the time he got me to the doctor three days after the beginning of my latest bout of screams, it was too late. The infection had started, spread, and set. The doctor got me on antibiotics, but by then, things were already growing gray. By the end of the week, my eyes had gone completely dark. And you want to know the funny thing? I stopped the constant crying. When my eyes shut, and I no longer had to take in the world at the pace I was consuming it, I became a quiet, cooing baby.

"My parents were never the same again. They spent the rest of their lives haunted by their guilt. My father felt guilty for putting me off; my mother felt guilty for sleeping through the start of my blindness. I think those few days shaped the rest of their lives. How they treated me. How they treated the children who came after me."

"How do you know all this?"

"My father told me before he died. He had one of those unburdening moments on his deathbed. He thought he'd find some peace after telling me, but he didn't. It had been stuck in him for too long, and scraping it out would have taken a lot more than a confession in the days before his death. It's not a pleasant thing to watch an unpeaceful death, especially when the person suffering the violence is your father.

"I think this is the last book I need to write. To write it means being more truthful than ever before. But it also means that I must negate everything I've written. The beginnings of my life have been based on a half-truth. My father died when I was twenty-eight. I'd just published one book then. Over all the other books, I never corrected what I wrote. I kept the lie intact."

"Why aren't you writing it?"

"To write the book means showing that my parents had been careless. And that I've lied about it for years."

"They weren't careless. They were just tired."

"What do you mean they weren't careless? I lost my eyes."

"And you weren't lying. The fact that you couldn't talk or write about it is the subject of the book."

The themes of the book as I imagined it—the complications of parents and their children, the truths we hide from in order to survive—were themes I had wanted to explore. But the fact was that I didn't have either the life or the imagination to make a story of it. Anil did.

"Does Mira know all this?"

Anil shook his head no.

I didn't understand why he trusted me with this information.

"You have to write this story out," I said. "It's *the* story."

As we walked out of the stadium at the end of the game, Anil seemed to be in good spirits. The Catholic obsession with confession suddenly made sense to me. I'm still not sure what Anil was to me at that moment. From the outside, I must have looked like the caring son, the late twentieth-century version of the boy carrying his father on his back, from village to village.

Over the next few days, Anil tried to dictate the story to me. He'd talk for ten, twenty minutes, trying to construct sentences, and then get tired and distracted. I had no idea about the ways of successful writers, but I'd imagined these long stretches of time when the *stuff* would just come out in long sentences and paragraphs.

But after a week of working three hours a day, we barely had five pages. It would have been one thing for them to be polished. But they were just scraps and afterthoughts.

"Let's take a little break," Anil said, as I read him some of the pages. "We'll try again next week."

He was self-preserving enough to not say that he was giving up on the project. He was taking a break, and soon he would return, refreshed and ready to go.

But then he added, "It's garbage."

I couldn't understand why the story Anil had told me at the baseball game didn't translate to paper. It was the most riveting thing I'd heard from him. But with paper and pen in front of him, something shut off. Perhaps it was the story. Too painful. Perhaps he was just too old to get through the rigors of completing one sentence, placing a period, taking a slight breath, and then moving on to the next sentence.

The following Monday when I came over, Anil was nowhere to be seen. Since my arrivals were regular and on schedule, I would knock on the front door and walk in. Anil would usually be sitting having his tea. But he wasn't there that day.

"Anil?"

"Rakesh," I heard my name faintly coming from the back of the house.

"Anil?" I said and walked toward the voice.

"I'm in here. In the bathroom."

"Take your time."

"No," he said. "You need to come in here."

"Is everything all right?"

"Just come in here."

I slowly opened the bathroom door. Anil was sitting on the toilet, with his pants down at his ankles. In the few days since I'd last seen him, he looked the way he did in New York. He'd not shaved, and the graying salt in his beard made him look like the near dead.

"How long have you been in here?" I asked. Something was wrong.

"Half an hour. Maybe an hour. I can't get up. I sat down to pee because my legs were feeling weak. But now I can't get them to work."

The state of his speech and thinking was in far better shape than his body.

"What should I do?"

"Just give me a hand. Lift me up and then pull up my pants. I can take it from there."

I went up to him, placed my arms under his armpits, and tried to lift him up. He was dead weight.

"When I count to three, try to get up."

At three, I lifted him up. For a second, he was stable, but then he got a little wobbly.

"If you can just pull my pants up, it'll be the last thing I ask."

I kneeled down and took hold of the pants and the simple white, cotton underwear beneath it. And as I lifted them up, I tried my very best to keep my eyes averted from his groin, for his sake and mine. And my head was turned away as I was pulling up his pants, but at the last second, I turned right to it, and there was this small bit between his legs. Age was savage in its destruction, but I'm not sure it could shoulder all the blame.

As soon as I got his pants buttoned properly, we started walking out of the bathroom. For the first few steps, he used my arm, but then he started walking on his own.

"I have no idea what just happened," Anil said. "I couldn't walk and now I can."

"Should I call a doctor?"

"No, no," Anil said. "Let's just call it a day. I want to take a little bit of a nap."

"Maybe I can just sit here while you sleep."

Anil shook his head. Me sitting and watching over him was not an option.

"I'll call you later," Anil said. "Let's take a little break from work for now."

After I left the cottage, I walked with my bike for a few blocks. I couldn't disentangle my sorrow for having witnessed such a rapid decline in the man and my confusion about who exactly the man was.

Several days later, Mira called on my cell phone. I was in my apartment, working on a research paper.

"Rakesh, I really need to see you. Are you home? Can I come by?"

I looked around my little studio and remembered their place in New York. I lived on the third floor of a carriage house, in a studio apartment that was barely three hundred square feet. It had sloping ceilings, smoky glass along one strip of wall, and yes, shag carpeting. When I'd first rented it, I'd imagined myself writing a novel here and then, years later, being able to remember that I'd written my first novel in a tiny third-floor apartment. I'd written no such novel, and now that spring was accumulating, the apartment was hot, cluttered, and uninspired. I didn't want Mira seeing the place.

"I'll come to you," I said. "Just tell me where you are."

"I don't want to be out in public. Tell me how to get there."

She was knocking on my door within ten minutes. She'd been crying, and when she walked in, she came right up to me and started weeping as deeply as she had laughed that first time we'd really talked. We sat on the edge of my futon.

"It's over," she said. "I can't do it anymore. You've seen him. He's getting worse. He needs my help more than ever to get around, to do everything. And every passing day, it feels like he's finally giving in to the blindness more and more. And I'm happy to help him, but he doesn't want the help. I knew the age difference when we got together, but now it feels like I am caring for my dying father. I don't even mind this, but he yells at me constantly. Just now, he was barking at me, daring me to leave, daring me to come here and complain."

Now I was sure Anil was, for whatever reason, pushing Mira toward me.

She cried in my arms, and all I could think about for the whole time was how desperately I wanted to kiss her, to strip her clothes off on this warm afternoon. Sure, she didn't know that many people in town. But she'd come to me for a reason.

When there was a slight lull in the crying, she pulled her head up and apologized.

"What is it with us? All we do is cry around each other."

There were tears all over her face, her eyes had puffed up, and there was moisture beneath her nose. I leaned forward and kissed her. She kissed me back with a certain enthusiasm and desperation that told me, at least for that moment, that this was all right. At the beach when we'd kissed, I could feel her hesitance. But now that the hesitance was gone, it was almost frightening to be at the cusp of something I had wanted for so long.

After she let me take all her clothes off, I couldn't help but think of Anil. He had her, but he'd never had the pleasure of watching her fleshy quivering breasts, the purple of her nipples, and the depth of the color between her legs. For a few seconds, I just looked at her.

"What?"

"Are you real?"

She laughed and then tugged at my hair and pulled me down. For a while, I covered her entire body with kisses and bites. Then I reached over for the pack of condoms I'd bought nearly a year before.

"No, no," Mira said and pulled me back.

It was a bit of recklessness on her part and mine. I'm not reckless. I wasn't then, and I'm not now. But at that moment, I was, and not because her naked body had shut off a part of my mind. I was reckless because I could have lived with whatever the consequence: a child, a burn. My parents were gone, I had no siblings. I was alone in the world, and I wanted a future.

After I was in her, I did my desperate best to think about why Pedro belonged in Flushing. After a minute, Mira got on top and arranged our bodies to maximize her pleasure. She buried her face in my shoulder, and all I could see was the ceiling above me. She went harder and harder, which felt good, but I sensed that she was trying hard to forget. When she came, she was far away, clearly unavailable. I wanted to pull out, but she pushed down on my bottom and insisted I finish in her.

As we lay on my bed afterward, she looked around the apartment.

"How do you live in such a small place?" she asked.

I knew that I was a diversion for her. But that didn't stop me from enjoying every second of smelling her skin and kissing her. I ran my fingers up and down her smooth thighs.

"Again?" I asked, half an hour later.

"Sure," she said smiling. "I forgot about the energy of the young."

The second time, she was more present and I was less nervous.

Just about the time we finished, Anil was on the other side of town. He was walking along the streets around the cottage he'd gotten to know well over the past months. He stood at nearly the exact place that he and I had stood that first time we went for a walk, identifying the cars that went by.

The driver of the truck that hit him told the police that he'd noticed Anil standing there, waiting, he thought, for the light to turn green for him to walk. He'd seen Anil as he was approaching, but he was quite high up in the cab of his Volvo truck and had not seen Anil step out onto the street in front of him just as he approached. He just heard the impact.

We were lying in bed when Mira got a call. The police had called the university, which called the head of the Center, who called Mira.

"I'm on my way to the hospital now," he said. "There's been an accident."

I drove Mira there, and all along, I assumed his legs had given out again and he'd fallen at home. He'd probably broken a hip.

When we got to the emergency room, there was a doctor and two police officers waiting for us. He'd died en route to the hospital. The injuries were far too severe. When they explained how he died, I had trouble comprehending it all. This was the stuff of other people's lives.

The police asked Mira why a blind man was walking by himself. This was the question everyone would want to ask. "He wasn't supposed to be," she said. "But," she continued, nearly spitting the words out, "he's not a child I can control every moment of the day." Neither of us mentioned, to the police or each other, that he knew those streets extremely well and had a freakish ability to identify the makes of cars by the hums of their engines.

The official word was that the death was an accident.

Over the next week, I helped Mira gather their things and arrange for the funeral and the cremation. We spent time together, but I could see that Mira allowed it only so that I could help her. She barely looked at me, and she shut down any attempt at conversation. Even though our sex had been a diversion for her, I still thought we could turn into something resembling the intimacy we had shared over a few kisses. But that possibility ended the moment we learned of Anil's death.

The funeral, which the Center hosted, was a minor literary event. His writer friends flew in from all over the country and said the things about him and his work that he'd started to doubt. Mira's parents came, as did two of Anil's sisters. I sat in the back of the campus chapel and listened. Mira sat up front, surrounded by friends and family. She didn't introduce me to anyone.

A day after the funeral, Mira was leaving for New York with her things, the urn of ashes, and the unfinished three hundred pages. There was a part of me that held on to the hope that Mira would ask me to come to New York with her, but I knew she wouldn't. She'd been through two marriages that ended badly, and she wanted nothing to do with another relationship for a good long while. She wanted nothing to do with me.

But she did ask me to drive her to the airport.

For the first twenty minutes, we made small talk about all the people who had attended the funeral and how Anil's editor had spoken so eloquently about the light hand he needed in editing Anil's work.

"Tell me not to feel bad about how things ended," I finally said as we got closer to the airport. "Because I feel horrible."

"Who would you be if you didn't?"

It was not the answer I was looking for, but it was fair.

I kept my eyes on the road, but I knew her tears were coming. I could feel them collecting in her eyes. She'd not emoted in front of me at all since Anil's death.

"It makes me sick to think about him that day. I let him die alone." She paused. "*We* let him die alone."

She had her guilt and would have to contend with it. I had mine as well. But I know now, as I did at that moment, that we didn't share the same guilt. The two of them had spent some good and bad years together, and I'd simply walked in right as it was starting to stay bad. My arrival was the beginning of their end.

When we got to the airport, I didn't bother to park the car. At the curb, I assumed I was seeing her for the last time. She didn't suggest I look her up the next time I was visiting my father. She just gave me a hug and disappeared into the terminal and her sorrow.

For nine mostly good months, I thought I was living this ideal life that was far more glorious than the lives occupied by my fellow graduate students who spent their days and nights diligently reading and preparing themselves for a mediocre career of teaching and minor publications. I thought I was better than them and had therefore completely abandoned my friends and acquaintances. And so right after Mira walked away from my car, I felt a ferocious loneliness. Anil was dead, and my hands were not clean; the woman I thought I loved barely noticed my presence. And I had no one to talk to about it all.

A month later, I received a large package in the mail. First-edition hardcovers of every book Anil had published. Each was inscribed to my father, dated two days after Christmas. A note from Mira accompanied the books.

"I have been meaning to send these to you. I hope you are keeping well. M."

There was no mention of what Anil might have left me. But then again, he'd already given me a gift. I thought it was an afternoon with the most beautiful woman in the world—the one thing I had wanted more than anything else. But now I know it was so much more.

I stayed in town for the summer. I'd already been thinking about leaving graduate school. I had two more years of scholarship money left. I decided that I would stay, do the minimum work necessary, and take the time to write the things I wanted. At the end of the two years, I'd walk away with three hundred pages of my own.

After Anil died and Mira left, I sat at my desk, with the sloping ceiling in front of me, for a good part of the next two years. With death and the memory of a perfect woman in my mind, I started quickly writing about Anil, Mira, and the true nature of his blindness. When I ran out of steam with that, I turned to my family and me. Writers and painters talk about productive years. These were those for me. The work had no polish, but it was during this time that I removed layer after layer of memory, bits of conversation, glances, fights, and on and on from my mind. Pages and pages. I'd blink and there would be five hundred words in front of me. In the years that followed, as I left graduate school, moved into my parents' apartment, and picked up little teaching jobs here and there, I went back to these early pages and began the work of cleaning them up, transforming gobs of memory and experience into neat, contained bits of narrative.

I wrote stories and essays. A half-finished novel. Then a novel I finished and then revised. Roughly six hundred pretty clean pages on my hard drive. I published a story, then two. Even a third. I felt like I was on my way. I had fancy degrees, had rubbed shoulders with famous writers, and I thought I'd look good in author photos.

It was during this high moment of promise in my writing life that Helen moved back to the Bay Area, partly to start a job after finishing law school in New York and partly to give us one more try. She had fled, I had fled, and now we finally turned toward each other in the safe comfort of a cottage in Berkeley. She liked me writing; I liked her lawyering. I didn't marry her for her family's money or her future earning potential, but knowing these facts allowed me to feel a little better about devoting all this time to a career that offered so few guarantees.

But just as quickly as I'd arrived at a place where success seemed imminent, I ended up at a place where success abandoned me. The luck ran out; the stars stopped aligning. No matter how hard I tried knocking on various doors, the world was no longer interested in my work. The stories sat there, as did the novel.

As I was writing, I couldn't imagine a time I wouldn't. I'd deferred that act for so long that I felt I was constantly making up for lost time. But then one day, six years to the day after Anil died, I stopped. There was no ritual page burning. Just a cease in activity from the exhaustion and frustration of feeling ignored. We had a child and wanted another. Helen didn't say I needed to think about alternative careers. She didn't need to.

I put out some feelers in the finance world I'd rejected years before, but it had moved on. It had no place for a man who'd been very ambitious in his twenties but had nothing to show for it except a few minor publications in magazines that had died out.

And so I did what anybody who's failed at his chosen career does in a boom time: I took the real estate exam. After apprenticing and then slowly building up a clientele, I caught the last six months of the housing craze. I'd have one open house and ten offers over asking. I made gaudy money. We joined a tennis club. I bought Helen a real wedding ring. I took up golf in a nonliterary kind of way. I thought I'd transitioned well. Our first child came when I was still writing. The second one was conceived when the commissions were rolling in. When the second arrived, the market had begun its steep decline, and we thought we would get a little help here and there from Helen's parents. But in one catastrophic year, they lost too much money in the market. They were now living fragilely on their nest egg, high above Central Park.

Unable to sell houses, and with an aborted writing career behind me, I felt gutted. Sure, money hadn't bought me happiness, but it had made me comfortable. I desperately looked for something that would kill the feeling that my young life had come to nothing. For a few weeks, I'd be fine. But then I'd dip into something dark. I didn't sleep past two a.m.; I snapped at my kids for being kids; I fought with Helen constantly. On the freeway, I'd drive at forty-five and be completely unaware of the cars zipping past me. And then I'd arrive back into the light for a while.

We fail at the things we want to succeed in. I did. Pure and simple. I kept thinking that spending all this time with a blind man would help me see things in a way I hadn't before. And for a while, as I drove around in a silver Range Rover I couldn't afford, needing to keep up the appearance that business was good, showing couples house after empty house, I looked to Anil's death as a warning about getting too overwhelmed by failure.

During the day, I went to work, and Helen juggled her twenty-hour-a-week job at a small law firm with looking after our younger son. She managed him and the woman who came in to take care of him a couple of times a week when she was working. The older one was in preschool, and Helen and I took turns picking him up and dropping him off. Given the opportunity, she would have earned more than I could working full-time, but she quietly said that she preferred the part-time work and the time with our boys.

Since the day the younger one was born, the older one has been in a tizzy about the whole thing. Occasionally they play together, but mostly the older one just whacks on the younger one. I'm no psychologist, but when I see them together, I feel like I'm raising brotherly archetypes. I'm just not quite sure which one is going to go all Cain on the other. I try to manage them with every bit of patience I can muster. But I honestly feel that every time I yell at them for something or the other, or I'm not around because I have to show houses that will not sell, I'm fucking them up in the same way Anil's parents and mine had done before me.

Balancing out the craziness are the boys themselves. Beauties. They get it all from their mother, which is what I like to say when people remark on them. It's a bit of false modesty, but it also annoys me a little because I know it's the truth. The only substantive things they've received from me are the width of my shoulders and the heft of my footprint.

They are a lot of energy, and at the end of the day when they should be tired, they are like the penguins we like to go see at the zoo: swimming around frantically, bumping into each other, taking a momentary rest by swimming backward. And then starting all over again.

One night recently, I promised Helen that I'd put both of them to sleep. I had had work events the previous couple of nights, and she needed a break. And so at seven p.m., I started the process. I took the younger one into his room, placed him in his crib, turned on *Diamonds & Rust,* which he likes to sleep to, and sat down on a chair next to the crib. There was a time when we could just lay him down and he would fall asleep. Now, he rolls around and talks to himself and insists we stay there with him. I sat on the chair next to him with a flashlight and the *New Yorker,* avoiding the short story and reading everything else prodigiously. The process lasted nearly an hour. An hour of cute but frustrating energy.

I went from the younger straight to the older. We got into bed, and I read him *Tintin*—the same books that I had read when I first came to America and was learning English. Then we turned off the lights. For twenty minutes, he just thrashed around the bed as if being awake was as important to him as water might be for a fish.

At nine p.m., I emerged from his room, fighting off sleep so that I could have some quiet downtime, a luxury that had become scarce in our life. I had to get up at six the next morning. If I gave myself about seven hours of sleep, that left me with a sweet two hours to do nothing.

I took a shower, poured myself a hefty bit of bourbon, and worked through my options. *SportsCenter?* Julian Barnes? The first option was winning out more and more, and I hated it. I had vowed not to become this.

"Can we talk finances?" Helen asked just as I turned on the TV.

While I was putting the kids to bed, Helen had been doing paperwork and growing increasingly agitated.

"Can we not?"

"I know you don't like talking about this, but we need to. Things aren't lining up."

We had moved into a house the previous year that we'd bought before it came on the market. Perks of the job. It was a little bit beyond our price range, but it was perfect for us. In the Berkeley hills with a view of the Bay Bridge; great public schools; a yard for the brumbies. And so we bought it, thinking that the housing crisis was other people. And now we were having trouble keeping it all together.

"I don't want to talk about this right now."

Talking about it made me nervous. And nervous was not how I wanted to spend my two free hours of the day. And then I would have trouble sleeping. And sleeping was already an issue. I'd hinted to my doctor that I wanted sleeping pills, or at least antianxiety pills, but he'd subtly refused, saying that I needed to first work on my "sleep hygiene." A shower, a bourbon, and sports highlights was what I'd come up with.

"We have to. I'm not getting enough hours in. And your houses aren't selling as well as they should."

"You think I don't *fucking* realize that?"

Helen had a look of deep worry on her face, perhaps perplexed at the series of decisions she had made over the years that led to this particular evening. She was frustrated at me and at the situation. And in these moments, I would look at her, and for one passing second, I would have no recognition of this woman whom I spent so much time with, whom I loved so much.

For the next ten minutes, we talked about finances. I did my very best to show that I was listening, but my mind had already shut off.

"I need to be out tomorrow night."

"Not again, Rakesh. I'm exhausted."

"It's the only time they can show me the house. If I don't have listings, then I can't sell more houses."

"I know. I know."

Helen and I have always been understanding of each other. But we do have tense moments, and we try to keep the knives away. But sometimes they slip out. And in these moments, it's hard not to fantasize about going all Rabbit on her and the boys.

The next evening, I didn't have clients to meet. Instead, I ate a quiet Mexican meal by myself, with two beers, when I would have usually gotten the fresh watermelon juice. Properly fortified, I walked several doors down from the restaurant and into a neighborhood bookstore that I visited often when I was in college, then hoping that one day I would read from my book there. Five minutes before the start of the reading, the place was completely packed and full of chatter. The medicinal qualities of the beer now came in quite handy.

A week before, as I had been reading the paper at an empty open house, I came across a review for a book by Mira Trivedi. *The Blind Writer*. She was still going by her married name. Even before I started reading, my heart was beating wildly from having seen her name and from seeing the book that I had tried to write. For years, I had attempted to tuck Anil away, beneath the everyday concerns of work and family. And now, images of him in his chic sweaters came right back, along with the guilt surrounding his death. I could only get through the first paragraph of the review before I had to put it down. "From tragedy comes art. But in the case of Mira Trivedi, tragedy has brought forth luminescence."

For the first time ever, I canceled the open house I had scheduled for that afternoon and drove around for a while, unsure of what to do with myself. I ended up at the bookstore, bought Mira's book, and saw a sign for her reading the following week. I laid the book on the passenger seat as I sat in the car. It was the object of my envy, but it was so much more. I had my version of events, and this was hers. I assumed I was in there.

I found a seat toward the back, just as the reading started. I had not yet seen Mira in the store and wondered, or perhaps hoped, that they were going to announce a cancellation. But then I saw her, appearing through the crowd, standing just to the left of the podium. It was the first time I'd seen her in nearly a decade. From that distance, it didn't look like she had aged. It was a chilly night, and she was wearing a black wraparound shawl. She had that look of funereal glamour.

The store manager gave a brief introduction and then invited Mira to come up. There was loud, sustained applause. Obviously people had read the book and the glowing reviews. She went up to the podium, placed the shawl carefully on a chair next to her, and flipped through her book to find the page she liked, all before she looked up.

"This is a funny thing," Mira began, sounding tentative and looking visibly nervous. "I've been waiting so long for an opportunity like this, longer than you can imagine. To have written a book, to get it published, to have people read it, to be here. In all that daydreaming, I never thought that I would have a fear of public speaking. But I'm slowly getting used to it. So bear with me."

She scanned the audience as she spoke, and it was then that she and I finally made eye contact. I felt all the muscle and bone holding me together go slack. Mira looked a little confused and then went back to her book, flipped to a different page, and started reading. Now I was sure I was in there.

She read a long section about how she and Anil first met at a party at Columbia. The book was written as a novel, but it was in essence the exact story she had told me years before, but now with far more evocative language and the tone of an aggrieved, wise woman. It was told in the third person, and here is where she succeeded in a way I'd failed. The sections where she got into Anil's mind were dazzling and true. I'd spent enough time with him to know that when she read from his point of view, I thought I was hearing Anil himself. She got Anil's balance between not seeing and seeing too clearly just right.

I didn't hear most of the reading. I spent the time imagining what I was going to say to her afterward. Helen often made good-natured fun of me when I was nervous about talking to someone. I had a tendency of practicing the lines quietly to myself, with my lips moving but the voice barely audible. I caught myself doing that as she got through the section about Anil's smoothness when they first met.

"She'd always believed that a man's confidence could be seen in his ability to hold eye contact. While Amar didn't have that option, he left no doubt of who was in charge."

The questions after the reading were about Anil and Mira's life with him. She did her best to ground all her answers in the lives of fictional Amar and Maya, insisting that this was a work of fiction. Even after his death, most people were still interested in the logistics of being blind, and not with the work itself.

As she signed copies, I flipped through large books filled with arty black-and-white photographs of naked women. This was my guilty pleasure when I went to bookstores. Thankfully I'd moved on to a volume on American Expressionism when she walked up to me.

"Rakesh," she said and gave me a long, untentative hug. Her hair still smelled of lavender. "Have you read it? That sounds bad to bring it up immediately. Barely a hello. But I knew that somewhere down the line we would see each other and have this conversation."

"I haven't. It's just been . . ."

"Don't worry," she said, stopping me. "I don't mind if you haven't. You know you're in there."

"I was hoping I was. To be honest, I'm a little nervous to read it."

"You're white. Rob."

This bit of information made me spill out something between a laugh and a cough. Helen and I had had some small issues here and there with race, particularly in relation to raising our kids. And now Mira had reduced me to what I feared was happening to me and to my children.

"It just worked better," Mira said, shrugging her shoulders. "Greater conflict."

"Anything for art. But Rob? Did I rob you of something?"

"That's a conversation that needs a drink."

"I was hoping you had time for one."

Mira walked away for a moment and spoke with an attractive younger woman who had been speaking to the store manager. They chatted for a few minutes, and Mira pointed toward me and touched her arm. "That's the real Rob," I imagined her saying. "I have some explaining to do."

"You'll have to drop me off at my hotel after," Mira said as she walked back up to me.

As we were leaving the bookstore, I thought she might introduce me to the woman she'd spoken to, but we just walked out.

"Can we go somewhere quiet?"

Quiet was fine. But I lived in the area, and we had a lot of friends around. Where could I take her where one of them wouldn't see us? Helen and I were open and honest about most everything. She knew about Mira and me getting together as Anil died, and she wasn't a particular fan of this part of my life. But I needed to see Mira after all this time, to gauge how I would feel about her and to talk about Anil, and I simply couldn't tell Helen about it.

We walked to my car, and the first thing Mira noticed were the baby seats in the back.

"How old are they?"

"Four and two. Boys and pure madness. You?"

She shook her head no.

"Why not?"

I knew I shouldn't have asked the question, but it just came out before I could stop it. I could hear Helen's voice: don't ever ask a woman why she hasn't had children.

She paused and considered what she was going to say. "Mothering is not right for me. And besides, my baby-having years were after Anil's death. And those were lost years."

I had been imagining this reunion for so long, but now that I was in the middle of it, I wasn't sure how to proceed in the conversation. I felt nervous and jittery.

"Who did you marry?" Mira asked.

"A woman I dated early in graduate school. For a few years, we danced around each other. But I knew the moment I met her that we were going to get married. It just took us a while to get there."

"That sounds romantic."

"I would have married you if you'd let me."

Mira just smiled. "You know my history with marriages. I wanted to spare you."

"What are your thoughts on tobacco?" I asked as we started driving. A drink would calm my nerves, but a cigar would give me something to do with my hands.

"I don't mind it."

"There's a great place where we can have a drink and maybe I'll have a smoke. You seem to have a lot of fans, but I suspect none of them will be there. You can smoke in this place because they zone it as a tobacconist."

Helen and most of her friends hated smoking, and I thought this was the last place I'd see anyone we knew.

"That smells good," Mira said when we walked in ten minutes later.

It was a Tuesday night, and the place was empty. At the counter, they served port and Guinness on tap, and there was a small walk-in humidor. I bought a light cigar and got two glasses of port, and we found a quiet seat in a corner away from the door.

"Anil used to smoke cigars occasionally, and I miss the smell. He'd sit in his office, listen to baseball, and smoke."

Through the years, I had tried to work through the complicated parts of my relationship with Anil. It was nice to have this image of him smoking and be reminded that we had spent some wonderful time together.

For a few minutes, we caught each other up on the simple details. She was still living in New York, but in a different apartment. My mother was still sleeping a lot, and though I didn't see much of her, my feelings about her had softened. Her only real crime, I had realized, had been in wanting to live a life of her choosing. My father had died a few years before of a massive heart attack that finished him off even before he had a chance to feel the pain in his arm. He and Ruth were away for a weekend on the Hudson, and they'd just finished a perfect lunch of carrot soup followed by coq au vin. Together, they had become foodies.

"I'm so sorry to hear that."

"He had this thing he used to say. That sons don't come into their own until their fathers die. I suppose he meant that his death would be his final gift. I don't think I've come into my own, but it has certainly forced some issues."

I was feeling guilty about talking about something so intimate with someone other than Helen. And it made me terribly sad to think about my father, whom in many ways I had pushed away for much of my adult life. I'd kept looking for a father who would understand me and my ambitions on some deep level, and all along, he had been there patiently waiting. I'd just assumed that he would be around longer.

"Your parents still good?" I asked.

"They just keep ticking along."

"I could never tell whether Anil resented them or not."

"He was just perplexed by their happiness."

"That's funny you say that. Just when I started working for Anil, he asked me this question that has gnawed at me for years."

"About being happy?" Mira asked. "That was his thing. The question almost sounds simple and naïve, but it was the question he most wanted to answer in himself. I'm guessing he didn't like the answer the older he got."

"That must have hurt you a little."

"That's what I thought for years. But I made the mistake of thinking I could save him. All his women made that mistake. Nothing was going to save him. He liked asking the question because I don't think he was capable of happiness himself. He tried desperately but just couldn't get there."

This was Mira's conclusion about Anil's death, and she sounded like she believed it. There was authority in her voice, perhaps after a decade of uncertainty. I wasn't quite there yet.

"Did you think that last book he wrote was bad?" I asked, feeling nervous about her answer.

In my mind, I had some vague order I wanted to follow in talking about Anil, but instead I just dove right into the middle.

More than anything else, more than having slept with his wife as he roamed the streets alone, this issue had weighed heavily on me. The fact was that my criticism was not just about the writing. I'd stupidly thought that he would hear my concerns, realize that his life with Mira was spoiling his writing, and then leave her. I'd be there in the wings, ready to scoop her up.

"I did. And if you think your criticism pushed him over the edge, don't. He'd been on that edge for a while."

For my sake, I wanted to believe this.

"Trust me, Rakesh. I have worked through this longer than I want to admit. Anil made his own decisions about his life."

"Did he know about us?"

"He seemed to know everything. I think he knew starting on the car ride home after seeing your mother. He always assumed someone younger would take me away, and he probably thought the live version of you was better than the person he was creating in his imagination. But I don't think he cared that much. He was angry about being blind, and the writing was the consolation, the payback he thought he deserved from the world. Everything else faded away. That doesn't mean *I* wasn't important, that *we* weren't important, but there were limits."

I took a big sip of my drink. I'd tried to bury Anil away because he was simply too much to work through.

"Are you happy?" I asked, blowing out a little smoke. I didn't smoke often, but I liked it when I did. The smell of tobacco on my fingertips made me feel older, more world-weary.

"I am now," Mira said without stopping to think about it. "I'm in a good relationship that works. Nobody's cheating on anybody. I went younger this time."

The beautiful young woman from the bookstore suddenly flashed through my mind. I wanted to ask the question, but this time I didn't.

"I still don't understand why I married a man thirty years older than me. I have a perfectly good relationship with my father. If I'm brutally honest, I thought he would make me into a writer. And ultimately he did, but the cost was way too high. Sometimes I wish I'd never gone to that party.

"This wasn't the book that I set out to write when you and I met. All those afternoons when you were with Anil, I would go to this café and work earnestly on stories about growing up Indian in very white New Jersey suburbs. Stories about my father taking a train into the city every day and my mother staying home and maintaining a perfect house. But there was just nothing happening with the stories. I was writing about a life I thought I wanted, not the life I had. *The Blind Writer* was the story I had to write. It just took a long while. And I'm happy with it."

She took a sip of her port.

"I really look forward to reading it," I said. "Can I ask how it ends?"

"A tragic accident," she said, looking straight at me.

"OK."

"So what about you? Are you still at it? In a funny way, that story of yours put me into a deep funk for a while. The writing itself. And how much Anil loved it."

"You know, I gave it a shot. A genuine shot. But it didn't work. It gives me a pit in my stomach to say it. It's strange to have such a long-standing ambition and not see it become reality. I wasn't looking to be rich and famous. I just wanted to have a book or two that I could show my kids when they got older. To say, 'This is what I was doing when I said I had work to do.' I think this is why Anil's question has stuck with me. I have a good marriage, kids whom I love, a house with a view. By most standards, it's a bounty. I shouldn't need anything else. But of course I do."

"If it's any consolation, the writing didn't work for me for years. Even with all of Anil's contacts."

I needed to hear that.

We sat there for a minute, both of us taking sips of our drink. There was something more I needed to say, the substance of which I had been thinking about for years but the words just now crystallizing.

"I just want you to know," I began, my voice suddenly cracking. "I want you to know how much I loved spending time with Anil. He respected me and asked me my opinion on things when I was just really a kid. He was good to me when I really needed it. Seeing you, I realize how much I miss him. And how much his death has hung over me all these years. I didn't need a father either. But perhaps he needed kids. My father carried around those books you sent for a while, and then I got them after he died. I still pull them off the shelf now and again and read a few pages. The writing is good, and good over so many books. What more could he have asked for? He had a long, successful career that now takes up a chunk of a bookshelf. He did what he set out to do when he was young. It's remarkable. I've always wondered if he thought he'd failed because he couldn't get that last book done. But that isn't close to failure. He lived a good, full life. My father lived a good, full life. Love came to them both late, but it came, just not when they expected it. I suppose that's the mystery and beauty of it all."

My eyes had started watering, but Mira's were flooded.

"I loved him more than I've loved anyone," she said. "At the end, that's all there is to say about him."

We'd gotten through our first drinks, and I offered to get another round.

"It's been so long since I've seen you," Mira said, "but I'm exhausted. I've been traveling for a few weeks, and we're going to LA tomorrow. Do you mind if we start heading back to my hotel?"

I was glad she said this. In one way, we could have kept talking for the rest of the night and into the morning. About Anil, about the two of us, about Rob, about writing. But at that moment, I felt satiated. We'd done the necessary scraping of old wounds, shared things about our new lives. More could be said, but nothing else was needed.

"No problem," I said. "I have an early morning. And the later I'm up, the earlier the boys seem to wake."

I'd barely smoked half the cigar when I put it out. We headed back to the car, and on the way to her hotel, we talked about the easy things. Her life in New York, mine in California. But mostly we just drove in silence. At one point, my hand was resting on the gearshift, and Mira reached over and placed her hand on mine and kept it there until we reached the hotel.

"It was nice seeing you again," Mira said when I stopped the car. "I'm sorry I didn't get in touch after you left me at the airport. I just needed to disappear. But I'm glad we've had a chance to reconnect. I'd love to meet your kids sometime. And your wife."

I appreciated the offer, but I knew that a meeting like that was never going to happen.

"Good night," I said.

Mira leaned across and gave me a kiss on the cheek. This was how our troubles had originally begun. A simple, chaste kiss. But this time, it felt a little motherly. For years, every time Helen and I had a problem, I'd turned to Mira in my mind and imagined a different life. But now that I'd spent an evening with her, she seemed like a relic, a mark of my past, a beautiful thing with some of the sheen worn off. I was still jealous of this book she'd written, and I still found her alluring. But all that didn't matter.

The moment she was out of the car, I rushed home to Helen and the boys. Maybe the older one would still be up. I opened up the moon roof to let in the cool night air and lightly held on to the hope that maybe one day, the universe would align and the gods would smile and that I'd be able to write about Anil and Mira with the right amount of humor and loss. And as I drove, I looked up and stole a few glances at the stars and felt like the light from above was lifting me upward.

ACKNOWLEDGMENTS

I would like to thank the many people who have helped make this book: the readers and editors who greatly improved the stories—Ryan Black, Barnaby Conrad, Willard Cook, Lacy Crawford, Joe Crespino, Carol Edgarian, Gretel Ehrlich, Elizabeth England, Gina Frangello, Jolie Hale, Scott Herndon, Tom Jenks, Julia Mitric, Aaron Peters, Rajiv Vrudhula, and John Weir; Keith Scribner—for his friendship, incisive reading, and steady guidance; my colleagues in the Department of Asian American Studies at the University of California–Santa Barbara, who have created a welcoming place to teach and write; Paul Spickard, who pointed me in the right direction at the right time; Erin Cox, who has been a great supporter of this book; Masako Ikeda at the University of Hawai'i Press, who has so thoughtfully guided me through the publication process; the two anonymous reviewers of the book; to my mother Ragini, my two sisters Uttara and Meeta, and Andy and Yvonne Neumann, all of whom have been so supportive through the fluid process of book writing; to Ravi and Ishan: a book for your shelf; and to Emilie Neumann, who has heard about and read each of these stories over and over again—a deeply felt gratitude.

ABOUT THE AUTHOR

Sameer Pandya was born in India and grew up in California. He earned a BA in history from the University of California–Davis and a PhD from Stanford University. He currently teaches literature and creative writing at the University of California–Santa Barbara.